Praise for the Safe Harbor Medical ® Mysteries

The Case of the Questionable Quadruplet

"Love the mystery and medical setting interwoven to tell a great story. Lots of twists and turns and plenty of suspects. The end is unexpected and the reveal compelling."
—Sandy Penny, SweetMysteryBooks.blogspot.com

"This is a wonderfully written mystery with lots of twists and turns that kept me glued to the book."
—Online Reviewer Jo-Anne B

The Case of the Surly Surrogate

"A very clever mystery where emotions and feelings ran deep making for a truly beautiful read."
—Pauline Michael, NightOwlReviews

"Attention cozy mystery readers: Jacqueline Diamond's second Safe Harbor Medical mystery only gets better! 5 Stars."
—Mary Castillo, author of *Lost in the Light*

The Case of the Desperate Doctor

"Filled with mystery and suspense from start to finish. The book will satisfy any mystery buff.
—Roslynn Ernst, InD'tale.com

"I was hooked from the beginning."
—Evie Drae, blogger/reviewer.

Books by Jacqueline Diamond

Safe Harbor Medical ® Mysteries

THE CASE OF THE QUESTIONABLE QUADRUPLET
THE CASE OF THE SURLY SURROGATE
THE CASE OF THE DESPERATE DOCTOR
THE CASE OF THE LONG-LOST LOVER

More Mysteries and Suspense

AND THE BRIDE VANISHES
DANGER MUSIC
ECHOES
HIS SECRET SON
THE EYES OF A STRANGER
TOUCH ME IN THE DARK

Safe Harbor Medical ® Romances

THE WOULD-BE MOMMY
HIS HIRED BABY
THE HOLIDAY TRIPLETS
OFFICER DADDY
FALLING FOR THE NANNY
THE SURGEON'S SURPRISE TWINS
THE DETECTIVE'S ACCIDENTAL BABY
THE BABY DILEMMA
THE M.D.'S SECRET DAUGHTER
THE BABY JACKPOT
HIS BABY DREAM

The Case of the

LONG-LOST LOVER

Safe Harbor Medical ® Mysteries

Book Four

Jacqueline Diamond

Published by K. Loren Wilson
P.O. Box 1315, Brea, California, USA

More information about the books and the author is available at www.jacquelinediamond.net.

From the Author

The process of writing and completing a novel requires research, editing and feedback. I'm grateful for the input of friends, fellow authors and subject experts.

For his invaluable advice, I want to thank Orange County Sheriff's Investigator Gary Bale (retired). I'm also grateful to my Beta readers, Deborah Golub R.N., and Marcia Holman R.N., and my critique group, Orange County Fictionaires. Also, a tip of the hat to experts who generously answer my questions: D.P. Lyle, M.D., novelist and forensics expert, and Paul Hoag, Senior Deputy Coroner in Orange County, California.

Welcome to the fourth Safe Harbor Medical Mystery!

Jacqueline Diamond
Brea, California
2019

In memory of Joyce Froysland Wilson,

and in honor of all those who battle

Parkinson's Disease

CHAPTER ONE

As it turned out, the woman was real.

Not a figment of my colleague's misbehaving perceptions. Not a delusion sparked by the misfires in his brain.

Real. Vaguely familiar. And disturbing, especially when encountered in this particular house.

Around seven p.m. on a Sunday, I'd received a call from Dr. Jeremiah Schwartz, who, like me, practiced obstetrics at Safe Harbor Medical Center. In a low voice, he'd urged me to pop over to his house.

"Eric, there is a woman present." Despite his hurried manner, he spoke in his usual stilted way.

"And?" I'd prompted, reluctant to abandon an evening of sprawling alone on the couch, catching up on medical journals.

"I am uncertain she is real," Jeremiah had said.

There are two questions I've learned not to ask my lanky colleague. They are: What the hell are you talking about? And, Why me?

I simply said, "Explain."

He cleared his throat, always a monumental task considering his long neck. "She appeared at my front door, requesting to rent my spare room."

"What's unusual about that?" I grumbled. With Jeremiah, there was no point in soft-pedaling my irritation. When he isn't focused on work, the noise in his head dampens his ability to detect nuances.

"Although I obtained permission from my landlady to seek a housemate, I have not advertised," he informed me. "Also, my visitor neither telephoned nor messaged nor rang the bell. Through the front window, I spotted her on my porch. She claims to be a local ob-gyn, yet I have not heard of her."

Safe Harbor may be a small town, but "local" encompasses a large area. Richly populated in every sense, Orange County, California is home to many doctors.

"What's she doing right now, while you're on the phone?" Delusions would, I presumed, suspend themselves when they became inconvenient, unlike real women. Or men, for that matter.

"She is measuring the room with a tape," he'd said. "Please Eric. I have no one else to ask."

Whether intentionally or not, he'd tapped into my weakness. I suffer from a misplaced hero complex, leaping to the aid of those perceived to be relying on me. My sister-in-law, Tory, claims it indicates a massive ego.

"I'll be right over." It was a short drive, and a mild end-of-summer evening. Also, as he'd indicated, who else could he call?

Jeremiah trusts few people with his diagnosis of schizophrenia. A successful physician and a high-functioning member of society, he deserves respect for overcoming the constant challenge of his disease, in my opinion. Not everyone would view it that way.

Downstairs, I explained that I had an errand to run. Tory and her father, Morris, both of whom had migrated into my house during the three years since my wife's death, barely glanced up from their ferocious game of Go Fish at the kitchen table. Their ability to ignore me was among their more endearing qualities.

From my home on a bluff with a marginal view of the harbor, my electric car cruised inland. Traffic being light, I arrived within minutes at the cottage-lined streets of Jeremiah's neighborhood.

I angled into a vacancy at the curb near his bungalow. In the lingering daylight, the blue walls and cream shutters glowed. Alongside the porch, bird-of-paradise plants thrust up orange-and-lavender spikes.

In this place, less than six months previously, another doctor had been found dead. Following a painful and complicated investigation that delved into the long-term consequences of sexual abuse and a subsequent attempt at revenge, she had been laid to rest. Her nurse, to whom she'd willed the property, had leased it to Jeremiah, who was unperturbed by lingering emotional overtones.

An instant after I rang the bell, he opened the door. Dark, piercing eyes regarded me from a height several inches above my own. He wore a pressed shirt and creased slacks, and appeared freshly shaved. He had always been fastidious, even when we met in medical school at Harvard more than a dozen years earlier.

This being my day off, I had thrown on jeans and a polo shirt. Not that I cared what impression I made on the lady in question. I had only to sweep my gaze across her, confirm or deny her existence, and depart.

Inside, the broad front room had gained fresh curtains since I helped Jeremiah move in. The worn carpet remained, and from the built-in cabinets at my left to the fireplace on my far right, only bare bones furniture and an entertainment system saved the space from nakedness.

"I am grateful for your assistance. I shall summon her." My colleague swung around and called, "Hello? Doctor?"

In the hallway, floorboards creaked, and a young woman appeared. She was quite tangible, with long, ice-blond hair and dark-red lipstick. "Sorry. I didn't mean to take so..." She eyed me as if a snake had slithered into the room and she was considering chopping off its head. "Dr. Darcy?"

"That's right." She did look familiar, but I failed to put a name to the face.

Jeremiah smiled, no doubt relieved that she was real. "Eric, this is Dr. Piper Blanchard."

"Blanchard," I repeated. Now, *that* rang a bell. More of a ring tone from ages past. Then it hit me. "Nicole's sister?"

"Yes." A crease formed between her eyebrows.

Nicole was one of the few women I had ever dated, and that was more than a decade past. Aside from that, my romantic history had been simple to the extreme. As a teen-ager, I fell in love with one girl and, aside from a short breakup, stayed with her through marriage and unto death.

During that separation, I'd connected with Nicole Blanchard, a passionate, volatile med school classmate. The affair had flashed across my horizon, as intense as a comet and as quick to burn out. A short time later, she'd left school, citing a desire to help her cancer-stricken mother.

Dimly, I recalled meeting this younger sister when she visited Boston. While I rarely forget a face, Piper had left little impression. However, I gathered she took a keen interest in me. More antipathy than interest, judging by her scowl.

"How is your sister?" I asked.

"You should know," she said.

"I beg your pardon?"

"Anybody care for coffee?" Jeremiah interrupted, as if we were chatting idly. Which, to a man oblivious to social cues, was the case.

We both declined. Piper wrapped her arms around herself, shivering despite her sweater.

"How did you hear about my extra room?" Jeremiah inquired, before I could quiz Piper further about her odd remark.

"From Brandy," she said.

Brandy was the nurse who'd inherited the house. "How do you know her?" he asked.

"I work with her."

The situation clicked for me. "You're the new ob-gyn in Chuck Kane's office." Although Chuck has admitting privileges at Safe Harbor, he sees his regular patients in a suite in nearby Newport Beach.

"Brandy is your nurse," Jeremiah summed up. "This indicates you are filling Alison's position. Are you aware that she owned this house and was discovered dead in the bathroom?"

That ought to dash any interest in renting, I mused.

"Dark histories don't bother me," Piper replied. "How about you, Eric? Or maybe they appeal to you."

I'd had more than enough of innuendoes. "Is there a problem about Nicole?" Perhaps, unjustly, she blamed our breakup on me. In fairness, people often recall past incidents differently, depending on their perspective, but I wasn't the one who'd called it quits.

"You might say that. She's been missing for nine years."

"What?" Although my former lover *had* had a wild streak, people don't vanish for such a long period without good reason. Or bad reason. "Under what circumstances?"

"The last anyone heard, she was heading here to talk to you."

What nonsense was this? "I think I'd remember if..." A

memory tickled, a phone conversation that had dropped from my awareness because it was unremarkable and had occurred at a distracted moment.

Vaguely, I registered Jeremiah inviting us to sit down, which we did—him and me on the sofa, Piper on a plastic resin chair. Thankfully for my jumbled train of thought, he resumed addressing his potential housemate. "I was acquainted with your sister, also."

Her attention shifted to him. "How?"

"We were all in the same class at med school," he told her. "She had a drinking problem."

He'd noticed that? Jeremiah was full of surprises.

"Yes, she did," Piper conceded. "How well did you know her?"

"Only slightly," he said. "She and Eric dated after he and Lydia broke up. She and I dated then, too."

"You dated my sister?" Her hands clenched in her lap.

"No, I dated Lydia. But I was never the man she loved." An unaccustomed wistfulness crept into his voice. "After a few months, we returned to our normal relationships, Lydia with Eric and me with my studies. I do not know what became of Nicole after she left school."

"But Eric does." Her gaze drilled into me. "Isn't that true?"

"I don't have a clue why you assume that." However, despite her irksome attitude, I supposed any insights might prove useful. "She did call me about nine years ago. I'd forgotten."

"When was that?"

I provided the exact date.

"Good memory," Piper snapped.

"Not really," I said. "It was the night before my wedding."

"That would be a memorable date," Jeremiah agreed.

His guest leaned forward angrily. "Why didn't you help

her?"

She appeared to have an entire mountain of assumptions, while I had only an anthill of facts. "With what?" I said. "She didn't ask for help."

"That's why she came here!" Piper flared. "Was she too inconvenient? Just got in the way of your wedding, I suppose."

Far from it. Nothing could have stopped me from marrying the woman who'd been my soul's mirror since junior high school. But, contrary to Piper's belief, her sister had made no request of any kind. "What would she have needed? Money?"

"Quit playing games!"

"It would be more productive," Jeremiah interjected mildly, "to allow Eric to describe what happened, rather than to debate what you assume."

The man had a logical mind. It made him an excellent diagnostician and, in this case, a sensible moderator.

Piper straightened, her back rigid. "Well, what did happen, doctor?"

Probing an amorphous lump of memory, I teased out the point at which the phone rang. I'd just returned from a pre-wedding dinner party, relieved to tug off my tie and suit jacket. I'd been staying in my father's house—this one—in the downstairs bedroom during my residency. My soon-to-be wife had shared an apartment with friends, both of us saving money for the future.

"It was after ten and I was tired," I said. "When she told me she was in town and asked to meet the next morning, I explained I couldn't because I was getting married."

"I'm sure that cheered her up," Piper said.

I ignored the gibe. "She congratulated me and apologized for intruding. I asked why she was in town, but she seemed in a hurry to get off the phone. She did mention she'd been living in Juneau and that her mother—your mother—had recently died."

"That's it?" Piper pressed. "Nothing else?"

"Not that I remember," I said. "Was she in trouble?"

"You could put it that way," Piper muttered. "No one ever saw her again."

While I regretted being unable to help, I didn't understand the hostility. If only I were trained in interrogation like my friend Keith, a police detective. Still, I did diagnose diseases, a more or less similar process. "What symptoms... I mean, what kind of trouble?"

She stared past me. "I'm not sure."

"Why not?"

"Nine years ago, I was living in Seattle," Piper said. "We didn't communicate much."

I applied more pressure. "How long before you figured out she was missing?"

"Six or seven months." The words dragged out of her. "When I called to tell her I'd been accepted for my residency at U-Dub, her phone was out of service."

Mentally, I translated that she'd stayed in Seattle to specialize in obstetrics at the University of Washington. "Did you try to find her?"

"Well, of course!"

"How?"

With a visible effort, she reined in her ill temper. "I asked around. She'd sold the family restaurant to pay Mom's medical bills. Friends and co-workers said she'd packed her stuff and driven off."

"And no one had heard from her?"

"Not that they told me." She glared. "It's not like I had any reason to panic. I kept expecting her to get in touch, and then I was working crazy hours at the hospital. It wasn't until I came up for air the next summer that I got really worried."

"Did you hire a detective?"

"Naturally! What do you take me for?" Her nostrils flared. "He charged me a bunch of money for exactly zip."

"No credit card use? No cell phone use? What about her car?" I'd learned something about how private investigators work since my sister-in-law became one.

"Which part of zip don't you understand?"

She was losing her temper, and I might soon lose mine. Time to wrap this up. "What brings you here now?"

"Not that we aren't glad to see you," Jeremiah put in.

Piper weighed her answer carefully. Too carefully? "I ran into a cousin who'd seen my sister shortly before she vanished."

"She had information?" Jeremiah inquired in the same bright tone.

She nodded tensely. "She remembered two things Nicole told her. That she was coming here to see Eric, and that she believed she was in danger."

"This cousin waited nine years to share this?" I didn't bother to hide my skepticism.

Again, the woman paused before answering, as if to measure her words. "She had no idea Nicole had gone missing. They weren't close, and my sister was always a little flaky."

True. "What kind of danger?"

"She didn't specify." Grimly, Piper added, "But she named you. You've admitted she contacted you."

"If she felt threatened by me, why would she come here?"

"To confront you," Piper responded. "She was never the type to let people push her around."

Neither am I. I tamped down my frustration. Obviously, Piper believed more had happened between her sister and me, either in Boston or nine years ago, than was actually the case. "Confront me about what?"

"Quit lying and tell me what happened to her!"

Jeremiah spoke up. "In my observation, Eric never lies."

"Thank you." I reminded myself that having a loved one disappear under puzzling circumstances could fray your judgment. "Have you filed a missing person report?"

"Yes, in Juneau. It went nowhere," Piper said bitterly. "It's up to me to get justice for her."

"But why relocate to Safe Harbor?" Jeremiah asked. "Did you not already have a practice in Juneau?"

"In Anchorage, actually." Piper tugged at her pencil-slim skirt. "I had personal reasons for leaving Alaska. Then, right after I ran into my cousin, I read about this opening at Chuck's practice. It seemed like fate."

"How long have you been here?" I asked.

"A few weeks."

"Why not call me straight away?"

She stopped twitching. "I've had a lot to do, meeting patients, submitting my credentials to the hospital. I assumed I'd run into you before long."

"And now you have," I noted. "Satisfied?"

"With what?" she said. "You've told me nothing."

Except the date of my contact with Nicole, when she'd presumably been in town. Although unless someone checked the phone records, we couldn't be sure where the call had originated. "You've got everything I know."

"You could hire Eric's sister-in-law, Tory Golden," Jeremiah said. "She's a PI."

Bad idea. Tory, who'd worked with my friend Keith at the police department before joining a firm of private investigators, mostly operates out of my house. Having her dig into my personal history would constitute an invasion of privacy, as well as a conflict of interest on her part. Not that she'd hesitate to skewer me if the situation warranted it.

"She's your wife's sister?" Piper asked.

"My late wife's, yes."

She showed no surprise that I was a widower. I assumed she'd researched me in advance. "You get along with her?"

"A matter of opinion," I said.

"She must know you well."

"Too well." I wasn't convinced that would work in my favor. "You should choose someone more objective."

Dropping the subject, Piper swung toward Jeremiah. "How much is the rent?"

He told her.

"Great. I'm sick of living in a motel. Can I move in next weekend?"

Damn. I'd been almost certain she'd pass.

"I will email you a sublet agreement." Jeremiah took her contact data, shook her hand and saw her off. "You are frowning," he commented when he rejoined me.

"I don't like her," I said.

"It is natural to dislike people who do not like us," he observed.

"Very astute." Why direct sarcasm at him? None of this was his fault.

"Do you suppose she noticed anything odd about me?" he asked.

"You were fine." I didn't suggest he share his diagnosis of schizophrenia with her. She might pick it up eventually on her own, but until she did, discretion made sense. Even other physicians can harbor prejudices against the mentally ill.

Although acquainted since med school, Jeremiah and I had only become friends recently. After his and Lydia's brief involvement, I'd feared he might be stalking her when he followed my lead by applying for a residency in obstetrics at the University of California, Irvine. He'd bought a car identical to mine, got his hair cut by the same barber, and eventually rented an office in the same medical building as me.

Only later did he volunteer an explanation. While studying and practicing medicine, he had no difficulty concentrating. In private life, beset by mental phantoms, he'd floundered until he decided that, since Lydia and some of our colleagues liked me, he should adopt me as his template. As long as he behaved exactly as I did, he'd rationalized, he would appear normal.

Once he'd confided the truth, I'd stopped ducking through doorways to avoid him. Fortunately, he'd since gained enough self-confidence to reduce his copycattery.

As I took my leave, I hoped he wouldn't become too fond of his new housemate. Not only had Piper insulted me, I was certain she hadn't told us the whole truth.

Best case scenario: she'd find her sister, fast. But after nine years, that didn't seem likely.

CHAPTER TWO

When I strolled into the lobby of the medical office building on Friday, nearly a week later, a lab technician waiting for the elevator eyed me with suspicion. Given the gossip that had spread like drug-resistant bacteria through the hospital, I half expected her to opt for the stairs.

Instead, I took the stairs myself. Much more pleasant than enduring her uneasy company, and good exercise, too.

My awareness of the rumors had begun when I encountered questioning glances in the cafeteria. In the hallways, I noticed that conversations hushed abruptly as I approached, and lulls dropped like shrouds across normally gabby operating rooms.

Here and there, as the days passed, I had caught snatches of words. "Had an affair... woman disappeared... last person to see her..."

No, I wasn't! I wanted to shout. I didn't see her. And that affair happened before I got married.

But to respond would only add fuel to the fire. Once hysteria hits the gullible and the loose-lipped, it becomes unstoppable. Viral, indeed. If someone invented a vaccine, I'd volunteer to administer the shots myself.

Inside my office, receptionist Glenda was tapping rapidly on her phone. My nurse, the dedicated and gifted Farrah, cast her a stern look. After a tick of reluctance, the phone went into a drawer.

"Anything new on the rumor front?" I asked as Farrah handed me a patient's face sheet.

"Just the same nonsense," she returned briskly. "Except it's getting more exaggerated, like that game where people whisper a secret down the line until it's completely out of whack. No one with half a brain believes you cheated on your wife."

I had to snap my jaw into place before responding. "Because I didn't."

"Of course not."

Where had the gossip stemmed from? I hadn't spotted Piper at either the hospital or this adjacent building. Since the practice she'd joined was located a few miles away, there'd be no reason for her to hang around until she secured hospital privileges.

It hadn't required frequent reminders to keep Nicole Blanchard in my thoughts. My former girlfriend's face animated my mental screen: golden hair, amber eyes, ready smile. She'd had a keen memory for the gobs of data that med students need to absorb, which was fortunate, because she'd studied less than most of us. Breezy self-assurance had floated around her, the kind of surpassing confidence only a twenty-something can carry off without arrogance.

When I asked why she'd chosen to be a doctor, Nicole had said her father died in a hunting accident when she was fifteen. A restaurant owner in Juneau, he'd supplemented the family resources by hunting and fishing. Shot by accident in a remote area, he'd bled to death before he could be airlifted to a hospital.

"A lot of people in Alaska live in isolated towns," she'd added. "I'd like to save some of them." Her goal had been to specialize in emergency medicine.

Despite admiring her idealism, I'd had doubts about her temperament. Her vivacity often spun into exuberance, especially when stoked by alcohol, and she soon dropped out of our study group. Fundamentally unsuited to each other, Nicole and I had parted even before Lydia and I reconnected.

Yet for a while, in a Boston winter, she'd bloomed bright against the gray hardscape. Why had she disappeared? I kept replaying that conversation of nine years ago, seeking a word or tone of voice that might offer the key to where she'd gone or what danger she'd feared.

Had there been an abusive relationship? Nicole didn't strike me as the type to be easily intimidated. And if she'd reported threats or a stalker to the police, Piper's missing person report should have dredged up that information. Could she have killed herself? If she had, she apparently hadn't left a note, nor had her body been discovered and identified.

Why didn't anyone among her friends have a clue where she'd gone? If only they had searched sooner. By the time Piper set her PI on the trail, it must have gone cold. But then, she hadn't actually disappeared from Alaska, since her last known whereabouts had been in California.

Despite the troubling sense that I'd failed Nicole, I had to concentrate on my work. And there was plenty of that.

Originally a community hospital, Safe Harbor Medical Center still offered a range of medical services, including maternity care, general surgery, and pediatrics. However, during the past decade it had also established a world-class center for men's and women's fertility treatment.

Later that morning, I filled in for another doctor, performing egg retrievals and implanting embryos. Thanks to advances in microsurgery and embryology, eggs can be removed from a donor, fertilized with sperm from the husband/partner or a male donor, and grown inside the wife/partner or a surrogate. It's a complex business, and expensive, although the hospital offers an assistance program. Success rates have risen dramatically, and there is no joy to rival the birth of a much-desired, healthy baby.

Mornings like this aroused a mixture of longing and elation. Eventually, I hoped one of the children brought into the world would be my own. However, it hadn't happened for Lydia and me, and I had yet to meet another woman I could love.

For now, I substituted the privilege of bringing happiness—in best-case scenarios—to others. I was more fortunate, in my view, than those who specialized in performing these procedures, because as an ob-gyn with a regular practice, I shared the course of my patients' pregnancies and assisted in their deliveries.

At lunchtime, en route to the cafeteria, I paced alongside anesthesiologist Rod Vintner, a wiry fellow in his forties with gray hair bristling below a surgical cap. "Is it true?" he demanded. "Did you have flaming sex with an alien from Alpha Centauri?"

A strained smile at his wisecrack was the best I could manage. "What have you heard?" Rod's a magnet for ear-bending conversations in the O.R.

"Something about a missing old girlfriend," he said. "And a lot of speculation run amok."

"A woman I dated for a month or so in med school was last heard from nine years ago, when she called me for a casual conversation," I summarized. "That's all I know. Her sister might be spreading the rumors."

When I tossed out the name Piper Blanchard, Rod replied that he'd met her that morning in the company of Dr. Chuck

Kane. Her new boss must have helped her secure permission to treat patients here.

"Good-looking woman. Intense, but she didn't share any fabulous rumors with me, darn it," Rod noted. "Honestly, I've been hearing this crap all week. Seems centered in the cafeteria. At least, that's where it's the loudest."

"I may have lost my appetite," I grumbled.

"Eat, doc. You need your strength." He shooed me into the large, noisy dining room.

Spicy aromas drew me to the taco bar. Behind the counter, a fiftyish woman in a yellow uniform, her gray-laced dark hair restrained by netting, sneered as she added a dollop of refried beans. "Well, well, if it isn't the infamous Dr. Darcy."

Beside me, Rod tensed, and another cafeteria worker frowned at the serving lady, whose bar pin identified her as Y. Worth. Rudeness was out of place toward any customer, and doctors occupied a particular position of respect.

Who the hell do you think you are? nearly flew from me, but lashing out at a person in her position would be just as bad as what she'd done. I was well aware of my status, and of the moral obligation not to abuse it.

"You might want to watch what you say to my brother-in-law," commented another doctor, from behind Rod. "He's very good at disposing of bodies."

Leave it to Tory's younger brother to lighten the mood. Barry Golden, a urologist and men's fertility specialist, is my favorite member of our family. He's open, supportive and unfailingly kind.

"Yvonne's new here," put in the second woman in yellow.

In the glare of disapproval from all around, Ms. Worth ducked her large head. "No offense intended."

"Let's forget it," I muttered. *No offense taken* would be untrue.

I wondered why my personal history would interest a new employee. But some people act as if the entire world has enlisted in a reality show for their entertainment.

Barry went to join his usual lunch companions outside on the patio, while Rod accompanied me to a table. Although I would have preferred dining outdoors, Jeremiah was signaling to us.

We slid into place. "That woman has a loud voice," Jeremiah observed. "I did not hear Dr. Golden's response but I gather it was amusing."

I repeated it to him. He smiled.

"Here's what I'm thinking." Rod paused with his taco in midair. "A boxing match between Ms. Worth and Nurse Keely Randolph. Place your bets!"

Despite my reluctance to joke about an innocent party, I couldn't avoid a peek at a table from which several doctors and nurses were clearing their trays. Among them was Keely Randolph, R.N., a dour woman built like a Mack truck.

A few years ago, she'd accused the abrasive head of our fertility program of being arrogant and egotistical, descriptions secretly supported by a number of other staffers. She'd barely hung onto her job. While he'd since mellowed, she hadn't, much.

The ob-gyn she currently assisted left early several afternoons a week, freeing Keely to earn extra income, but she had little tolerance for picking up shifts with other doctors. For some reason, she respected me. While I didn't need additional help in my office, I'd had a painful experience with a dishonest housekeeper. To my surprise, Keely had offered to fill that role, and now moonlighted as my cleaning lady. She did an excellent job, and we got along fine.

Springing to her defense in a humorous situation might be overkill. Instead, I told Rod, "No bets. She might bruise her hands and quit working for me."

"Can't have that," he agreed cheerily.

Among those bussing trays to the conveyer, I spotted Chuck Kane. And when Keely turned to leave, a woman in a white jacket slipped into view from behind her.

Piper Blanchard's eyes met mine across the lunchroom. She rocked slightly, as if I'd fired an invisible salvo. The ambient din of conversation faded. People had noticed.

After disposing of her lunchware, Piper marched toward our table, thin and sharp as a scalpel. Did she have questions for Jeremiah about the weekend move? Surely that could be handled in a less public fashion.

Rather than watch her approach, I studied my refried beans. And decided not to eat the congealing lump, considering who had served them.

Adjusting her white coat, the newcomer occupied a chair across from me. "I want you to know that I'm not responsible for the gossip," she said. "Well, not exactly."

Was she responsible inexactly? And if so, how? Rather than get into an argument, I awaited enlightenment.

"I, um, guess I spoke out of turn." She hesitated.

"If you are indiscreet, it will not be acceptable for you to occupy my spare room," Jeremiah said.

"What?" Piper blinked. "No, you misunderstand. The gossip was, well, unintentional."

"You talk in your sleep?" Rod hazarded. "With a megaphone?"

A blush brightened her cheeks. "It was a stupid mistake." Her gaze skimmed my face, not lingering. "I've been staying at the Harbor Suites. You know the place?"

We all nodded. Within walking distance of the hospital, the motel leased rooms by the day, week or month. It was popular with out-of-area patients and their families, and offered discounts to long-term residents. It was also far superior to the town's other motel, which lay closer to the freeway.

"Being new around here, I hadn't met many people. I kept running into that woman over there." She indicated the hot-food station.

"Note that the witness has identified Yvonne Worth," Rod said as if addressing a courtroom. "You mean her, right?"

"Yes. I kind of over shared," Piper said. "About my sister and Eric. It never occurred to me she'd shoot her mouth off around the hospital."

"Some people have no respect for boundaries," Rod deadpanned.

"Now she assumes we're friends. She drops by my room and pesters me for more details," Piper said. "You see why I'm eager to move this weekend, Dr. Schwartz."

"Is it likely she will track you to your new home?" Jeremiah inquired. "I would not like to encounter this person in my front yard."

"She doesn't have a car. And if she shows up, I'll tell her I'm not allowed to have guests." Piper twisted a strand of her pale-blond hair. "Please don't change your mind."

Jeremiah thought it over. "I will sublet to you on the condition that any information you learn at my house remains private. That includes observations or conversations involving me or my friends. And that you entertain no unpleasant guests."

Her head bobbed. "As long as you don't object to my continuing to probe my sister's disappearance."

He turned to me. "Eric, would such conduct by my housemate pose a problem for you?"

While I resented her intrusion into my circle, separating Piper from that Worth woman was in my best interest. Besides, depriving her of her new home seemed cruel and pointless.

"Not at all. I'd like to get to the bottom of what happened to Nicole, too."

Piper tapped her fingers on the table. "Then you don't object to my hiring your sister-in-law's services?"

Before I could figure out how to phrase my objection, Jeremiah said, "Tory is an outstanding investigator."

"Good, because I dropped by her firm yesterday and signed a contract."

I nearly choked on my taco. Rod whacked me on the back, which was completely unnecessary.

Tory hadn't mentioned it to me. After a few swallows of water, I said, "I refuse to be interrogated in my own home."

"She promised to keep her investigation separate from your private life." Behind Piper's cool tone, I sensed her watching me closely. Did she believe I'd hidden her sister's personal effects in the attic? Or that I'd break under pressure and spew the truth of my homicidal guilt over the breakfast table?

"I'm not sure that's possible," I began.

"She assured me that she's a professional," Piper responded.

"Yes, but she's human."

"I already paid her a retainer." Before I could summon further argument, our companion excused herself and left.

Fuming, I resumed eating. The rest of my taco sank into a lump in my stomach.

"Charming woman," Rod observed dryly.

"Matter of opinion."

"I will keep an eye on her," Jeremiah assured me. "Just as I presume she plans to keep an eye on you."

"Thanks." His words hardly registered. I was too busy wondering how Tory imagined she could keep her inquiry apart from our home life.

I got my answer a few minutes later when my phone rang.

It was my nurse.

"Your sister-in-law is here," Farrah said. "You have half an hour before the next patient. Shall I send her away or ask her to take a seat?"

"Does she have a medical complaint?" I asked.

"She says it's private."

Yeah, I'll bet. "Show her into my office," I said. "I'll be right over."

*

When I entered, my tall, no-nonsense sister-in-law rose to shake hands as if we were mere acquaintances. I decided to go immediately on the offensive. "I presume you're here because Piper Blanchard hired you to find a missing person. Have you discussed this with Keith?"

The reference to her on-again off-again boyfriend failed to faze Tory. "I don't review my cases with the police unless there's good reason." She resumed her seat in an upholstered chair. No jeans or loose shirt today; her slacks and jacket suggested a business suit, and she must have applied half a tub of gel to subdue her frizzy chestnut hair. "Do you have knowledge of a crime?"

As I swung behind my desk, it occurred to me that I didn't recall Tory ever visiting me here before. Ironic, considering that her half-sister had chosen the décor, right down to the black-and-silver frames on my degrees and medical license.

Tory bore little resemblance to my petite, dark-haired wife, aside from the ability to skewer me with a stare. And their voices. Hearing Tory speak was like being touched by a ghost.

"No crime that I'm aware of," I returned shortly.

"Let's run through the story, shall we?" Her choice of words—story instead of facts—irked me. However, I could hardly fault her professionalism. "Mind if I record this?"

"Go ahead."

After she'd activated her recorder and identified the time, place, and persons present, I recounted my romantic involvement with Nicole Blanchard. It had lasted less than a month, I noted, and we'd drifted apart by mutual consent.

"Are you sure of that?"

"That's my perception," I said.

"Did Lydia know about this affair?"

No, I was running around behind her back like a complete jerk. "Yes. Just like I knew she was dating Jeremiah."

There was the briefest of pauses. "Dr. Jeremiah Schwartz?"

"Surely you were aware of that."

"Just confirming. What was your last contact with Nicole Blanchard?" she asked.

I repeated the details of her call and the request to meet the next day.

"Did you agree to it?"

"The morning of my wedding? Absolutely not."

"Do you have any witnesses as to your whereabouts after she contacted you?"

As in, had I run out and strangled her for inconveniencing me? *Stow the sarcasm, Eric.*

"Only my father," I said. "Unfortunately, he's dead." Dennis Darcy, M.D., had succumbed to a heart attack four years later. I was grateful that he'd lived long enough to be present at my wedding and had welcomed me into his medical practice.

The next question caught me off guard. "Do you play around a lot?"

"What?" I half-rose from my chair. "That's a hell of an implication!"

"We're simply establishing your romantic history." To me, her tension implied anything but indifference.

Damn it, the woman lived in my house. "You think you might have noticed me bringing home strange women."

"Please answer the question."

A devilish impulse seized my tongue. "Well, a couple of months ago at a medical convention in Baltimore, I had a few torrid nights with a fellow physician. Female, in case you're wondering."

I was almost pleased to see her momentarily at a loss for words. Almost, because I hadn't intended to share that. Also, because I wasn't proud of it, although I'd been unaware that my lover was engaged to be married. She hadn't worn a ring, nor had she mentioned her attachment until, on the last day of the event, I suggested we keep in touch.

She'd declined and explained why not, implying that having casual sex while betrothed was normal behavior. Ironic, since a doctor should be especially sensitive to both the physical and the psychological risks. But it hadn't been my place to lecture her, or to do anything more than say goodbye and be grateful at escaping from further involvement with her.

"And before that?" Tory asked.

"I've always been monogamous. Let's move on."

"Returning to the night Ms. Blanchard contacted you nine years ago," she said. "What did she state as the reason for the call?"

"She didn't specify, except that she was in town." Probably true, or how else could we have scheduled a meeting? "I supposed she was making introductory chitchat before getting to the point."

"Which was?"

"I'm clueless. She congratulated me and rang off." I wished now that I hadn't told her so quickly that I was about to be married. If only she'd had a chance to explain what was going on.

Tory stared down at her notes. Surely she hadn't run out of questions already. Rather, I got the impression she was building to something.

Finally, she looked up. "Did you know Nicole might have been pregnant when she dropped out of medical school?"

Oh, hell, no. I just stared at her.

CHAPTER THREE

"Are you messing with me?" I couldn't believe my sister-in-law suspected me of abandoning my own kid, and keeping this huge secret during my entire marriage.

"She didn't mention it?" Tory's voice quavered.

"No. Not in med school and not nine years ago. If she was pregnant, what happened to the baby?" He or she would have been about three years old when Nicole vanished, and would be twelve now. Was it possible that I'd had a child living all these years without me? "What did Piper tell you, and don't lay that client confidentiality crap on me. You brought it up."

"That's irrelevant. I can't repeat anything she told me in confidence," she snapped, a hard-nosed contrast to the trusting patients who usually visited my office.

"Piper's playing you," I persisted. "Playing me, too. If there's a missing kid, she should have opened with that. Did the baby die? Was it adopted?"

"She claims she doesn't know anything for sure." Tory clamped her lips tight, as if the disclosure had flown out of its own accord.

"You expect me to buy that?"

My sister-in-law appeared to be losing an internal struggle.

"She might be reserving information."

"Lying." I'd suspected as much.

"Being cautious."

Since this line of questioning was proving futile, I tried a different approach. "What about this danger she claimed her sister was in? Was there another man in the picture?"

"We're starting with you."

"Then you're starting with zip." However, more than anything, I needed the truth about whether I was a father. "Have you checked birth records in Juneau or wherever Nicole was living? What about the restaurant her parents owned? Even if it's under new management, someone might recall the family."

"I'll look into that," she said. "Depending on what the client wants."

It couldn't be that complicated to unearth the truth about whether Nicole had had a baby. "This cousin Piper supposedly bumped into, the one who pointed the finger at me," I pressed. "Who and where is she? Surely she'd know if Nicole had a kid."

"I'll follow up on all counts."

My sister-in-law's thoroughness could be counted on. However, that didn't necessarily mean she would share her discoveries with me.

My phone beeped with an alert from Farrah. "There are patients waiting," I said. "Keep me in the loop."

"That's up to..." Tory waved away the rest of the sentence. She'd never been one to waste words.

Since I preferred to keep this conversation corralled to my office, I pushed a little harder. "When can I expect to hear more?"

"Possibly never." After stating the time and other key data, she clicked off her recorder. "Nine years missing. Our best bet is to review Jane Does, although Piper claims she gave a DNA sample to the Juneau police."

I appreciated her sharing her next step. However, sifting through records of unidentified dead women wouldn't help if Nicole's body had been dumped in an unmarked grave. All too often, decades-old skeletons turn up in California's deserts and brushlands, mute testimony to ancient agonies.

We might never learn Nicole's fate. Now that Piper had raised the possibility of a pregnancy, this was my concern as much as hers.

For the rest of Friday afternoon, questions slunk in and out of my thoughts as I examined expectant mothers and new moms, addressed older patients' medical needs, and discussed fertility options. Most of the time I had no problem concentrating, but at unexpected moments, my brain leaped to what-might-bes.

Had Nicole borne a child? If so, where had he or she been all these years? Did I have a son or daughter being raised by strangers?

And what about that sneaky Piper? How could she be aware of a pregnancy yet ignorant of the result? Was she lying for some messed-up reason and, if so, what did she hope to accomplish?

Even if there was a child, nothing guaranteed my paternity. Nicole had been a heavy drinker and fond of partying. Also, we'd never promised exclusivity, although it hadn't occurred to me to date more than one woman at a time. Playing the field lacked appeal, and who had the energy, with that heavy load of coursework and clinics?

We'd taken precautions, plus she'd been on the pill, or so she'd told me. But accidents happen.

Finished for the day, I headed for the elevator. By now, I hoped Tory would be home. If she'd learned more, maybe I could shake or shame the details out of her. Or just growl at her. That might feel good.

From the fourth floor, I took the elevator, which was surprisingly empty at this pre-dinner hour. Had everyone left early?

On the second floor, Dr. Nora Franco slipped inside. Her expression brightened when she spotted me, not that there were any vibes between us. Nora was married—happily, from all appearances—with a little boy.

"Just the person I wanted to see," she announced.

"Oh?" Considering the gossip infusing the medical center, I wasn't sure how to take that.

"Leo and I are throwing a Labor Day party," she said. "We'd love for you to join us. Everyone brings food, so the more the merrier."

I'd attended a previous party at Nora's condo near the harbor, which I'd enjoyed, but we didn't often socialize. Was this a gesture of support? While I welcomed people to my camp, if I had a camp, I'm hardly the schmoozing and beer guzzling type. Okay, an occasional beer. Anyway, the reminder that this was a holiday weekend explained the early duck-outs by staff.

"That's kind of you," I said.

"Selfish, rather." Nora grinned. "There'll be cops all over the place, including your friend Keith. I get tired of sports talk and griping about politics. It'd be nice to have an alternate source of conversation."

Her husband, Leo, was a detective sergeant and Keith's supervisor. Interesting group. "I'm not sure I'm fit company," I admitted. "Grumpy these days."

"Yeah, I've heard the character assassination," Nora sympathized as the elevator doors opened on the lobby. "No pressure. You have my number, right? Text me if you can come."

It was a generous offer. "If I can, what should I bring?"

"Whatever's easy."

"I'll get back to you," I promised, feeling churlish for not leaping in with a "Yes!" But I'd been truthful about my unsettled state. Also, in our small town, there was no telling how far the hospital rumor-mongering had spread. My insertion into a social event involving Keith might tempt me to share more personal stuff than I wished to.

If I'd expected privacy at home, however, it was not to be. Outside the three-story Tudor-style house where I'd grown up, vehicles clustered like sharks feeding on a kill.

A boxy brown sedan bristled with in-your-face bumper stickers: "Ask Your Doctor—Not Your TV Commercial" and "Cancer Cures Smoking." Property of my housecleaner, Keely. A van lettered Golden Fine Foods Catering indicated Morris had returned from his rounds of delivering specialized dinners to customers. A tidy white Civic belonged to my father-in-law's catering assistant.

The only vehicle missing, I saw as I drove into the garage, was Tory's green sedan. Since she worked mostly from home, I wondered if she was digging through records of unclaimed bodies. Or out stirring up trouble.

Inside, a great room dominated the ground floor, beneath a skylight three stories above. I caught the scent of cleanser and, from upstairs, the whirr of the vacuum cleaner.

My favorite place is the kitchen, separated from the larger area by a counter. It's an enticing spot, with catering-quality appliances and a cozy table. The house also boasts a formal dining room and a breakfast nook overlooking the back rose garden, but we rarely use them.

My father-in-law, whose white chef's hat added a comical touch to his chubby frame, was transferring food from catering boxes into the large refrigerator. Although Golden Fine Foods has its own kitchen, office and tasting room, my household enjoys his leftovers. Especially me.

His uniformed employee, the seventy-something Helen Pepper, deftly positioned trays of goodies on the counter. She enjoyed using her graceful hands, freed by medication from once-crippling arthritis.

Helen's face tilted up at me. "Better eat, Eric, before Keely's new protégé tromps down here. She'll kill your appetite, not to mention snarfing down the food."

"Keely's protégé?" I didn't care for strangers in my house, and no one had mentioned that the nurse-slash-cleaning lady had acquired a sidekick.

"She's Keely's younger cousin." Morris swung around, nearly dislodging his hat. "We have plenty of food. I don't begrudge her a plate."

"I don't like her," Helen informed me, keeping her tone low. "She's rooming with Keely. If you ask me, she's a bad influence on my granddaughters."

Since the death of Helen's daughter—my friend Rod's ex-wife—a few years earlier, her two teen-age granddaughters had lived with their father and his warmhearted second wife. Keely rented a suite in their large house.

"I thought Keely didn't have any family." After surveying the platters, I sampled a spring roll. Crunchy and tasty.

"She took one of those mail-order DNA tests." Helen arranged a tofu wrap, plus steamed vegetables and green chips, on a plate for me. Since my mouth was too full for a thank-you, I ducked my head in gratitude. "Next I heard, she'd acquired a second or third cousin from Utah. Starla Randolph. Same last name and the DNA proves they're related, but if you want my opinion, that girl is a real pill."

"You aren't usually so judgmental," Morris commented.

Helen frowned. "I beg your pardon?"

"She's a bad influence, and she's a pill, whatever that means," he repeated. "That's two judgments in as many minutes."

"I'm seventy-seven years old. I'm entitled to my opinions."

"No argument there."

A series of thumps yanked my attention across the expanse to the curving staircase. A chunky young woman with pink-and-blue tinged hair was dragging down a vacuum cleaner.

"Doggone it, Starla, be careful with that!" From the second-floor landing, Keely hauled a bucket and a mop into view. "You'll damage the wood."

Pausing, Starla shook back her chin-length locks. Although I guessed her age at about thirty, she had the airy manner of a teenager. "Honestly, Cousin K, who would notice? I mean, if I had a place like this, I'd decorate it, not leave it practically empty. And boring!" She gestured over the great room where my artist wife had chosen subtle opalescent hues that shimmered in the light from overhead. "Imagine what you could do with splashy floral prints instead of this bland stuff."

I stiffened, and Morris gasped at this insult to his beloved stepdaughter. Helen's lip curled.

Finally, Starla noticed she had an audience. "Oh, hi, there." She marched down the rest of the way, making a show of half-lifting the vacuum cleaner.

Keely descended with more speed and smoothness than one might expect from her blocky build. "Dr. Darcy, I didn't realize you were home. Starla, I'm sure the doctor is perfectly happy with his house the way it is."

"He doesn't mind a little constructive criticism, though, right?" The young woman winked at me as she pushed the equipment across the floor.

I let the comment pass. In my experience, what people call constructive criticism is often thinly veiled hostility.

"I've always wanted to be a decorator," Starla rattled on, enjoying the attention. "Maybe I'll sign up for classes. What do you think, Cousin K?"

"I think we should put our gear in the laundry room." Keely pointed.

"Wow, look at that cute chef's hat!" Starla beamed at Morris as they rolled and clunked past us. "You're a caterer, right? Do you need an assistant? I used to work in a restaurant."

No one answered, since Helen was standing right there in her black-and-white uniform. With a roll of the eyes, Keely shooed her cousin around a corner into the laundry area.

"See what I mean?" Helen muttered. "No filter and no manners."

"She must have redeeming qualities," Morris said softly. "Keely likes her."

I wasn't sure about that, but cleaning is hard work, and I couldn't fault Keely for sharing the heavy lifting with her cousin. In fact, I decided to buy a second vacuum to store upstairs. Should have done that long ago.

When the two women returned, Morris invited them to eat. While I would rather he hadn't, there was plenty.

"If you don't mind, Dr. Darcy," Keely said.

"Of course not."

Based on Helen's earlier comment, I anticipated that Starla might show signs of compulsive eating, which can indicate depression and low self-esteem. However, she took no more food than the rest of us, and carried her plate to the table rather than graze at the counter. Keely settled to her right and, recalling my manners as host, I sat opposite with my half-empty plate.

"How long are you visiting Safe Harbor?" I asked Starla.

"Oh, I'm planning to stay. It already feels like home!" She smiled. "I love California. My family in Utah is a drag. They're always criticizing this and complaining about that. They won't let me have any fun."

She was here permanently? I wondered if Keely had taken that into account when she invited her newfound relative to stay with her. Checking her reaction, I noted a dour expression, but then, that was Keely's normal demeanor.

Helen, who stood scooping herself a bowl of almond-milk-based ice cream, winced. "What's your notion of fun?" If it involved hanging out with her teen-age granddaughters, I feared that bowl might go flying through the air.

"Where do people party around here?" Starla responded. "Is there, like, a singles bar, with loud music and cute guys? Cousin K, where do you pick up men?"

Coughing, Keely took a moment to reply. She'd never hinted at a social life or group of friends, not in my presence, although she demonstrated fierce loyalty toward her chosen few. "I meet folks where I work," she said.

"At the hospital?" Starla scrunched her nose.

"You might like the Suncrest Saloon." I recalled it as a popular spot that met the loud-music-plus-singles criteria. "They advertise theme nights, like Star Wars and karaoke."

"I'll check it out." She beamed at me. "But hey, if I worked at the hospital, I might meet rich doctors. What a kick! Why don't you hire me, Dr. Darcy?"

Heaven help us. Silence throbbed. The sense of being put on the spot reminded me of the rude incident in the lunch line—which generated an idea.

"Since you used to work in a restaurant, you could apply at the cafeteria," I said. The standards there must not be very high, judging by the loud-mouthed woman who'd insulted me.

Starla wriggled with excitement. "I'll put you down as a reference!"

"Inappropriate," Keely said. "Use my name."

"Thanks. I'll still help you with the cleaning. Hey, don't put the ice cream away!" Starla called.

Helen set it and the scoop on the counter. "It's right here."

If Starla landed a job at the medical center, she might prove an ongoing annoyance. Still, I enjoyed the prospect of her irritating the snot out of Yvonne Worth.

My ill temper fading, I dished out ice cream for everyone. Not a bad start to a holiday weekend, with the prospect of lots of private time ahead.

From the hall, I heard the front door open. Since Tory normally enters via the garage, I experienced a spurt of anticipation at the prospect of a visit from my brother-in-law, the only other person with a key.

"My office is around to the right," said that familiar husky voice, eerily like Lydia's.

"This is quite a house. Practically a palace." Even without the undercurrent of resentment in the woman's tone, I identified the speaker an instant before the pair emerged into view.

Tory had brought Piper home with her.

CHAPTER FOUR

From the entry hall, Piper glowered at me. What was she doing here? Since Tory updates her clients often, I didn't see any reason for this hostile woman to invade the premises.

However, the intrusion was partly my fault for allowing my sister-in-law to use my front studio as an office. While she could take clients to the agency that employed her, it was less than cozy, and sometimes a client didn't wish to meet at her own home or office. Morris had suggested installing a separate entrance, but there's no walkway on that side of the house, and the expense would be considerable.

When I got to my feet, Piper took a step backward. Against her pallor, dark red lipstick stood out like a bloodstain. I could have sworn she was afraid of me.

Fear wasn't the usual reaction I inspired, nor did it fit my self-image. However, my anger at her behavior undoubtedly showed on my face.

"Excuse us." Almost grudgingly, Tory added, "Hi, everyone." Since her curt attitude included her father, I didn't take it personally. "We'll be out of your hair. Just carry on."

"Wait." Clasping her purse to her side—everything about her was tightly wired—Piper lifted her chin. "Eric should hear this. He can join us."

My sister-in-law appeared to sort through several reactions before saying, "Are you sure?"

Her client nodded.

"Very well. Eric?"

Propelled by curiosity, I crossed to them, feeling four pairs of eyes drilling into my back. Ahead, Tory's look was colder than the ice cream I'd abandoned.

This better be worth it. A faint hope stirred, that Nicole's sister might come clean about what she knew, what she suspected and why she was intent on targeting me.

We entered a large room bathed by lingering daylight through a bay window. Several multi-media works on the walls, constructed of bits of glass and cloth fragments layered over achingly vulnerable photos of women, reminded me that this had once been my wife's workshop.

Tory sat behind the desk, lord of her small domain. I drew a padded chair for Piper and another for myself.

"Thanks," she muttered.

"No problem." In my impatience, I nearly blurted, *What's this about Nicole being pregnant?* However, I saved that for later. "Dig up anything, Tory?"

Piper drew a sharp breath. Tactless phrasing, I reflected, too late.

"Not yet." She flexed her fingers, as if they were weary from mousing through listings.

The other woman's shoulders remained taut. "Are there a lot of... records to go through?"

"There are about a hundred individuals of both genders currently unidentified in Orange County," Tory said. "The coroner's office works hard to figure out who they are, posting photos online including artists' conceptions of what they looked like. None of them match Nicole's description."

"That doesn't rule out other regions," Piper said.

"No, it doesn't. I've already broadened my search. Ever heard of the NamUs project?" My sister-in-law pronounced it Name-Us.

I had. Piper hadn't.

"The National Missing and Unidentified Persons System," Tory said. "It coordinates with law enforcement, medical examiners, and families. Since you filed a report in Juneau, I expect they've already done the legwork. I'll follow up, of course."

"What's next?" Piper still didn't indicate why she'd wanted me here.

"I'll be checking motels, car rentals, airlines, anywhere that might have records from nine years ago," Tory said. "I'm also posting on social media, like I told you. Photo, description, etc. Can't include too many details or somebody will steal her ID, which could create confusion."

Shifting in her chair, Piper slid off her shoes. They were slender and pointy, the kind that fatten podiatrists' bank accounts. "Any response?"

"A few loonies with conspiracy theories. Some vague stories of seeing a woman who might resemble her. Nothing concrete."

"What do you think, Eric?" Piper said.

Her question startled me. "About what?"

"My sister must have dropped a hint about where she was going or why she'd come here."

"Like I said, we barely spoke." A note of irritation defied my efforts to stay objective.

"Maybe you met with her for a few minutes? At a bar or whatever?" Her eyes fixed on me a little too directly, pupils wide.

Her intrusive gaze smacked of the tactics employed by manipulators. Even if her motive truly was to discover the truth about her sister, her attitude reeked of deceptiveness. Was this her normal conduct, or had someone coached her?

"That's why you wormed your way into my house?" I flared. "As I told you before, I didn't see your sister, nor did I set up a meeting. If you keep pushing me, I might start to believe you spread the gossip yourself."

"What gossip?" Tory asked.

"Half the hospital has me pegged as a serial killer." Okay, slight exaggeration, but not by much. "Blabbermouth here claims she over shared and didn't mean any harm. That's becoming less and less credible by the minute."

Piper shook forward a sheet of pale hair that half-curtained her face. "I told you, I didn't do it on purpose."

"You're hiding something," I pressed. "What about this pregnancy business? Was Nicole carrying a child or not?"

She swallowed, hesitated, and finally muttered, "It's just a possibility."

She'd floated that as a trial balloon? "You must have known if she was pregnant. You're her sister."

Piper moistened her lips. "I was in Seattle when my mom told me Nicole dropped out of med school. I didn't talk to my sister directly. We'd argued about how much she drank, so we weren't on great terms."

"Your mother didn't tell you about a pregnancy?" I said.

"She hinted."

"How do you hint at that?" Receiving no answer, I continued, "And you heard zilch during the next three years? You had no idea whether you had a niece or nephew?"

"Maybe she relinquished the baby."

"*Was* there a baby?"

"I told you, I'm not sure."

This woman's story had more holes than Morris's garlic press. "You expect me to buy that?"

She squinted in a shaft of fading sunlight. "If she had been pregnant, would you have stood by her?"

Stupid question. "Of course."

"Even if meant giving up your little princess?"

Tory and I both scowled. "Is that how your sister described Lydia?" I demanded, although the answer was obvious. "What did she call me?"

"A golden boy," Piper said bitterly. "Rich and handsome. Like everything came easy for you."

I had run out of patience with her snap judgments. "You mean aside from my mother dying of cancer when I was thirteen?" I hated using that as an argument, but it slipped out. "That's what drew my wife and me together in high school. She'd lost her father as well." To suicide, which was none of Piper's business.

She glanced toward the door. "That, um, fellow in the chef's hat..."

"My dad, not Lydia's," Tory said. "Are we done here?"

"It's just that..." Piper blew out a breath. "If Nicole was in danger, maybe her child was too. If she had one."

"In danger from me?" That made zero sense. "If I had a kid, I'd throw myself under a bus for it. It's unthinkable that Nicole should have kept that from me."

"If she did, I'm sure she had her reasons." Piper's hands trembled in her lap.

"Am I or am I not a father?"

A tick of hesitation, then: "Not." But she didn't sound like she meant it. Damn.

"I'll check the birth records in Juneau," Tory assured me.

"You'll do what I pay you to do!" Piper sprang up. "And nothing more."

If she didn't check those records, I resolved to hire a detective of my own. However, I might as well let Tory finish her investigation into Nicole's disappearance, rather than risk working at cross-purposes. Whatever got us to the truth.

"I'll do my job thoroughly and professionally," Tory said.

"If you can't produce results by next week, I'll no longer require your services," Piper flung out.

"I'm still working off your retainer," Tory said. "I plan to earn it."

"See that you do!" The fumbling process of sticking her feet into her shoes frustrated Piper's attempt at a dramatic departure. Once shod, she stalked out, barely acknowledging Tory's escort to the front door.

A quick return enabled my sister-in-law to confront me where the others couldn't hear. "Stay out of this."

As if I wasn't already splat in the middle of it, through no desire of my own. "It's not my fault you have a disagreeable client," I said. "I thought it was a bad idea for her to hire you."

"You didn't recommend me?"

"Not even close." Why had she assumed that? "It was Jeremiah's suggestion."

She hmmphed.

"So you don't have to thank me for landing you a client," I snarked.

"Sarcasm doesn't suit you." Tory hated losing an argument.

"Okay, I'll be straight. Why'd you bring her to the house?"

"She requested it."

"To accuse me of lying," I finished. "And harass me outside the hospital, where there might be repercussions." Our administrator takes a tough stance against rumor-spreading. While he'd most likely heard the latest, I presumed he was biding his time rather than risk fanning the flames by speaking out prematurely.

"You can hardly blame her. She believes you killed her sister," Tory said.

"She doesn't even know me!" I forced myself to speak in a low tone. We might be out of sight of the kitchen, but not entirely out of earshot.

"Those two things are not mutually exclusive."

"I have no idea what happened to Nicole, but I'm a little surprised someone hasn't strangled Piper by now." I regretted the words as soon as I spoke them. "Didn't mean that."

"Is that why you kept staring at her?" Tory demanded. "Because she's so fascinatingly strangle-worthy?"

"I was glaring, not staring."

"What color are her eyes?"

"Pink." They were gray. Why had I noticed that? "Don't tell me you're jealous."

My sister-in-law folded her arms. "I had no idea you'd dated anyone other than Lydia."

We were, I guessed, circling closer to the heart of Tory's crankiness with me. "Your sister broke up with me."

"Why?" Her tone implied that Lydia would never have done such a thing.

I leaned out to peer past the staircase. No sign of the cleaning staff or Helen, and Morris had his back turned as he arranged items in the freezer.

"She needed space. Yes, it's a cliché, but it was true." We'd had the conversation in a coffee shop in Cambridge. Lydia had moved to Boston when I started med school, taking a website design job to stay near me. Our relationship hadn't worked out as we'd hoped. Her dark eyes, brimming with sorrow, had fixed on me across the table. "We'd been joined at the hip since we were fourteen. She felt stifled and restless. Unsure about a lot of things."

"My sister was never unsure about anything." A subtle shift of expression transformed my kick-ass housemate into the gawky, insecure teen-ager she'd once been, in the shadow of her fire-eating older sister. Funny how, despite being taller and more athletic, Tory had shrunk next to Lydia.

"Your mother died halfway through our first year in Boston." Nelle had been killed in a car crash. "Initially, Lydia appeared to handle it well. But grief is like cancer. It can hide and burst out later."

"Do you always think in medical terms?" Tory shrugged off her own comment. "Never mind."

"She had trouble adjusting to your mom's death, and there were other factors," I told her. "People in their twenties are still figuring out who they are. Breaking up hurt me, but if Lydia needed distance, she was entitled to it."

"So it was goodbye Lydia, hello, Nicole," Tory said. "Golden boy. Not exactly inaccurate, is it?"

Piper wasn't the only person who viewed me that way, I had to admit. Thanks to my physician father, I'd inherited a house and a medical practice, and was spared the burden of college loans. I was male, healthy, and reasonably tall, and even in my mid-thirties, my light-brown hair showed no sign of thinning. Yet part of me remained the scrawny geek who was taunted in junior high, until I struck a mutual aid pact with my jock friend Keith. I tutored him, and he protected me.

But that didn't show on the outside. Most scars don't.

"You're in a foul mood," I said. "Are you really planning to work all Labor Day weekend?"

Tory brushed past me, en route to the food. "Yeah. Although I might take a few hours off on Monday for a party."

I had a good idea which party she meant. "With Keith?"

"None of your damn." If she added the word "business," it didn't register.

Left alone, I took out my phone and texted Nora my acceptance. Her gathering ought to be fun, relaxing, and maybe informative.

I needed to get out of my head and enjoy the holiday. If it annoyed my sister-in-law, all the better.

CHAPTER FIVE

Nora's bluffside complex overlooked the beach and, to the east, the marina that gave Safe Harbor its name. In the late-afternoon sunlight, I wedged my car into an empty space down the block and lifted out my box of baked goods.

Keith insisted that, contrary to popular lore, police didn't eat a lot of doughnuts. Tory swore they did. I played it safe with a selection of pastries.

The wrought-iron security gate had been left ajar. Inside, fronds and flowers mounded alongside the path. It was a peaceful setting, all the more satisfying, according to Nora, because she had bought her condo with a large settlement from her first marriage, after her wealthy husband dumped her for a glamorous younger woman.

Everybody in town knew the story, since Reese Kendall had served a term as mayor. He'd later been defeated based partly on his offense to family values. But as head of a technology company with an international reach and, more recently, as owner of the local newspaper, he remained highly visible.

From inside drifted the rumble of conversation, topped by two women yelling at what I presumed was a fumbled play on a televised game. One of the voices belonged to Tory.

In the din, the chime of the doorbell got lost. I was about to press the button again when the door cracked and a preteen girl with brown hair and eyes stared up at me.

Despite common sense, the thought that hit me was: *This could be my daughter.*

She certainly wasn't Nora's child; that would be the little blond boy of about six peering from behind her. He clutched a furry arm that looked like it belonged to a teddy bear. The bear, however, was absent.

"Hi," the girl said easily, as if she were an adult. In one hand, she held a human heart, shot through with red and blue blood vessels. Plastic, of course. "Are you a doctor or a cop?"

"I'm Dr. Eric Darcy," Finally, I placed her. "You're Fiona Denny, aren't you?" Her father, Alec Denny, was the embryologist in charge of the hospital's laboratories and, if memory served, owned a unit in this complex.

She nodded. "This is Neo. We're in the middle of an operation."

That would explain the heart and the arm. "Those don't come from the same patient."

"We're running a clinic for our toys. I'd be happy to show you the O.R.," Fiona said. "I'm dissecting a cadaver."

"Want to help me stitch on my bear's arm?" Neo asked.

"Maybe later." I hated blowing them off, but there were courtesies to observe.

"Hey, guys, thanks for answering the bell." Nora opened the door wide. "Eric, glad you could make it." She accepted the box of pastries with an appreciative smile. "Good timing. They're decimating the snacks and the grill isn't quite ready."

The long room, encompassing a living area with a big-screen TV as well as an open kitchen, would be comfortably spacious under normal circumstances. That is, when not filled with a bunch of guests sprawling across the furniture and clustered around a snack table.

"Sorry I'm late." The invitation had been for two o'clock and onwards. It was past four.

"No such thing." Nora grinned. "I'd introduce you around, but you probably know everybody." She raised the pastry box high as she led the way into the mix.

I made a quick tally of the guests. On the couch, Tory lounged with her sock-clad feet on the coffee table. Beside her, radiating the same tough-but-warm vibe, sat her friend Patty Denny, a muscular woman who also worked at Fact Hunter Investigations. I'd met her in another context, via her husband, Fiona's father Alec. A mild-mannered fellow seated beside his wife, he greeted me with a brief wave.

I caught no telltale breaks in conversation, no sidelong glances. Had Alec and the others heard the ugly rumors at the hospital?

Among the guests gathered around the snacks, my friend Keith stood out, familiar as my own face in the mirror. A former high school football star, he'd been forced to tackle a spreading waistline in recent years, a contest in which he was barely staying even, no thanks to the potato chips in his hand.

Nora's husband, Leo, a rugged fellow with a friendly air, nodded to me. He was carting a plate of raw burgers toward the rear patio.

Mentally, I slotted people into their relative positions. A police sergeant, Leo supervised Keith and another detective I recognized, a pale fellow in his mid-thirties named Trent Horner. He was about Keith's height, but lacked his command presence.

"Great choice of bakery," observed Betsy Raditch, the hospital's nursing director, as she dug into the box. "Best in the area."

"Too bad it's about to be torn down," Trent grumbled.

Although it was out of my way, I'd opted for Delicious Memories, a craft and gift shop plus bakery with high online ratings. Located next to the freeway, it was operated by a pleasant, sixty-ish couple—last name of Horner, I recalled. A sign in the window had announced the store was closing. "Horner. Any relation?"

"My folks," Trent said.

"Too much competition from the Cake Castle?" Betsy asked.

The suggestion evoked a shake of the Horner head. "Forced to sell. Threat of eminent domain."

"They're widening the freeway?" I hadn't heard about that. The government can only force the sale of properties for public use such as schools and roads.

"No, some vague claim that the public will benefit if the city acquires the land, then sells it to Reese Kendall, because he'll redevelop it and pay more taxes," the detective responded bitterly. "My parents can't afford a legal battle, so they sold it to him directly."

"Did he pay fair market value?" Alec asked.

"Supposedly. But not enough to compensate for their lost business. Or for crushing their dreams."

The mention of her ex raised a spark of attention from Nora, who paused while arranging hamburger fixings at the kitchen counter. It also drew frowns from Patty and Tory, who'd pried themselves from the sofa to snag pastries.

"That's not fair," Patty agreed.

"Little guys don't have a chance against that creep." A whine edged Horner's complaint. "I guess having mega-bucks means it's okay to push people around."

While I sympathized, I was beginning to regret not buying my pastries at the supermarket, simply for the sake of keeping peace. "Well, your parents are talented bakers."

"They built that place less than ten years ago," Trent went

on. "That ass plans to replace it with a boutique featuring his wife's beauty crap."

An uneasy silence greeted this remark. The second Mrs. Kendall, the one who'd stolen Nora's then-husband, marketed a line of essential oils and supposedly science-based skin-care products. Her company was small potatoes compared to Reese's firm, which produced medical and surgical devices, but its glamorous image had made a splash with Hollywood celebrities, according to my starry-eyed receptionist.

"He should buy that seedy motel next door," Alec said. "It's an eyesore, unlike your parents' place."

"If he wants it, I'm sure he'll get it," Trent muttered.

Fiona wandered over, trailed by her smaller sidekick. She reached for a pastry, then stopped with her hand in midair. "May I have one?" she asked her stepmother.

Patty shot a questioning glance at her husband.

"Sorry, Fi," Alec said. "Save your appetite for supper."

"Patty's having one," Fiona pointed out.

"Don't eat junk like I do, kid," Patty said. "You might end up like me."

"What's wrong with you?"

"High cholesterol and bad teeth. Are there any more éclairs?" She sounded perfectly serious.

"Got the last one," Tory told her. "Come on! We're missing the game."

Despite my sympathy for the girl, I admired Alec's firm parenting. What was my son or daughter eating? Who was taking care of their teeth? *If he or she exists.*

Piper had sworn I wasn't a father. Well, not sworn, exactly. Besides, her grip on the truth was highly suspect.

The conversation had dropped off, aside from groans at on-screen fumbles. "May I tour your operating room?" I asked Fiona.

"Sure!" Brightening, she led her little friend and me through the condo to the den, where a life-size plastic body lay on the floor. Its realistic organs had been placed neatly at the side. "I'm teaching Neo to perform an autopsy."

"That's impressive," I said. "Are you planning to be a doctor?"

"A medical examiner, to solve crimes." The girl knelt beside her study subject.

"How about you?" I asked the boy.

"I'm gonna be a detective," he said. "Or an astronaut."

"Very ambitious."

I hung around these entertaining characters, helping Neo master the art of simple suturing and praising Fiona's efforts, until a call from the front room indicated the burgers were ready. "Hungry, kids?"

"Red meat isn't good for you," Fiona said.

"I love hamburgers!" Neo dashed for the bathroom, splashed around for a few seconds, and darted out with his hands dripping.

"At least he has the right idea," my young friend informed me. "About washing, not about meat."

These kids were wonderful. A pang twisted my gut. If I had a child this age and Nicole had hidden him or her from me... I wasn't sure where to direct my anger.

Damn it, she must have traveled to Safe Harbor for a reason. What had she meant to tell me? What about the danger she'd feared—had it threatened the child as well? If only I'd kept my mouth shut a few minutes longer about my wedding plans, she might have explained.

By the time we washed up, others had cut a swathe through the burgers and fixings. Sensitive to Fiona's concern about nutrition, I contented myself with baked beans, potatoes and green salad.

The televised game having ended, I sat on the sofa, plate on lap. Others drifted between the patio, counter and dining table, their voices forming a pleasant buzz. I didn't focus on anyone in particular until Leo addressed me across the room.

"What's this I hear about you disposing of an ex-girlfriend?" the detective sergeant queried pleasantly, his deep voice hushing the chatter.

I barely refrained from scowling at his wife, who had presumably shared the gossip. My peripheral vision showed red patches suffusing Nora's cheeks.

Still, this unwelcome gambit might provide a chance to learn how the police would view the evidence at hand. "You'll have to ask Tory. She's representing the missing woman's sister."

"Can't discuss it," she responded from a nearby chair.

"If there's a woman missing in our jurisdiction..." Leo began.

"It's Juneau's cold case," Patty chimed in from the dining table.

"Aren't all their cases cold?" teased her husband. "It *is* in Alaska."

"Oh, *Dad*," Fiona grumbled. She and Neo had chosen prime spots on the floor.

"Does this Alaskan lady have a name?" Leo asked.

"I can't discuss a case," Tory repeated.

"Nicole Blanchard." I felt no qualms about breaching her client's privacy, especially considering how blatantly Piper had violated mine. "I dated her for about a month while I was in med school." Might as well spill the rest, so I did. The phone call the night before my wedding, the abbreviated exchange, and then, according to Nicole's sister, her disappearance.

It crossed my mind to mention the pregnancy issue, but why? It was too personal and probably a lie.

Keith paused partway through his hot dog. "Did you run out

and knock her off, Eric?"

I resisted the urge to respond with sarcasm. *Sure, I've got bodies stashed all over town.* No telling how a roomful of cops might react. "No."

"Did she strike you as suicidal?" Leo asked.

"Nothing seemed out of the ordinary." Since everyone was regarding me expectantly, I noted, "She didn't sound frightened or panicky. We had a brief, casual conversation. Although she suggested we meet, I figured she was in town for some other reason. If she actually *was* in town." I had only her word for that.

"And nobody ever heard from her again?" Leo asked. "She must have left a trail."

Tory folded her arms. "If I discover evidence of a crime, I'll be sure to let you know."

End of discussion, I hoped. I'd forgotten about Fiona, who was peering at her cell phone.

"According to this site on how to locate missing persons, you should track her credit cards and phone records," she said. "Have you?"

Tory sighed. Couldn't lash out at a kid, could she? Well, that depended on how irritated she got. "Naturally."

"Did she rent a car? Stay at a motel?" the preteen continued. "Hey, how about alerting the media? Maybe somebody will remember seeing her."

Oh, great. Getting *The Safe Harbor Journal* involved meant bringing in its shark of a reporter, a woman with a gift for blowing the smallest incident into a major scandal. I'd been in her sights before, and it was not a pleasant experience.

"If you were a dead body, where would you be?" Neo put in.

Tory stared at him as if he'd just said something important. Quickly, she averted her gaze.

"We don't know that she's dead," I told the boy.

"Maybe she's in the Witness Protection Program," Fiona suggested.

Alec chuckled. "My daughter watches too much TV."

"Me and Patty!"

"My daughter *and* my wife."

Nora appeared from the kitchen with a couple of pies. "Anybody ready for dessert?"

Despite having wolfed down pastries before dinner, everyone was eager for more. To my relief, the topic changed to the merits of apple vs. pecan.

A while later, the party broke up. "I'm heading over to the Suncrest Saloon," Trent informed the group. "It's Beach Boys night. Half price on piña coladas. Anybody care to join me?"

A few guests expressed interest. As people wandered out, Keith buttonholed me on the couch. "I wondered what was keeping Tory tied up. She never mentioned it involved you."

"I wish it didn't," I said. "Piper Blanchard, Nicole's sister, seems convinced I'm the bad guy in all this."

"Someone's accusing Dr. Perfect of wrongdoing?" my friend joked. "What a shock!"

"Nicole was always a bit of a wild card, but I hope she's okay," I said.

"Me, too."

On my way out, Nora stopped me. "I'm sorry about gossiping to my husband. I didn't mean to spread rumors."

I strained to be fair. "He has a legitimate concern."

"I don't believe that extends to putting my colleague on the spot while you're our guest," she said.

"He obviously disagrees."

"Leo and I view the world from very different perspectives." She smiled. "Keeps our marriage interesting."

Her son ran up. "Bye, Dr Darcy. I hope you didn't kill her!"

"It was nice meeting you, too."

Behind him, Fiona patted the boy on the head. "Of course he didn't, Neo. I just wish we had a body so we could figure out who did this."

"Thanks for inviting me," I told Nora, and escaped.

At home, I kept replaying the discussion, but I was operating in a void. No sign of Tory. Had she picked up a clue from something Neo or anyone else had mentioned?

No matter how expert we are in our field, we can't think of everything. Doctors often fail to spot a connection among symptoms that might lead to a diagnosis, and I imagined detectives did, too.

Connections. There were a lot of them in a small town like Safe Harbor. Nora, her ex-husband Reese, the newspaper with its muckraking reporter, Trent and his unfortunate parents. Yet how could any of these people be linked to Nicole?

After about an hour, Tory arrived. She paced in from the garage, her shoes dusty and her expression grim.

"What?" I asked.

Impossible to read the look she cast me, except that it wasn't encouraging. "I think I know where Nicole's body might be buried," she said.

CHAPTER SIX

I was being watched.

Across the cafeteria, Yvonne Worth swiveled to keep track as I slid into a seat beside Rod. While it might have been kinder to my digestion to turn my back on the woman, I preferred to keep her in my peripheral vision.

Why was this cafeteria lady preoccupied with me? Perhaps she lived vicariously through other people's scandals. Or, heaven help me, maybe she fired off inanities on Twitter and craved material.

The day after a holiday is always busy, and this one certainly had been. In addition to scheduled surgeries, I'd performed several C-sections that morning and then, in my office, seen a couple of last-minute patients worried about symptoms that had manifested over the long weekend. Since my regular mealtime companions were also running late, we were still able to lunch together.

Rod, who'd administered anesthesia during my morning operations, was toying with a small, bright-yellow plastic pig's head that fired soft projectiles. Judging by his twitchy manner, he was imagining shooting something harder. Presumably at

Starla, Keely's cousin, vivid as a Tweety Bird in her new yellow uniform, gabbing to staff as she dished out vegetables.

"It isn't enough I have to put up with that annoying woman in my own house?" he complained. "According to Keely, she just applied here on Saturday. Why couldn't she land a job a little farther away, like, say, Arizona?"

I got busy with my grilled cheese sandwich. If he ever figured out that I'd had anything to do with Starla working here, he'd be aiming those puffballs at me.

"According to Piper, the cafeteria staff has been shorthanded," Jeremiah reported.

How would the newest doctor with admitting privileges know such things? "Where'd she hear that?" I asked.

He shrugged. "She did not say."

We ate in silence for a while. My thoughts drifted to Tory's guess about Nicole's final resting place. With Piper's approval, she'd taken this supposition to the man without whose permission nothing more could be done. That man was Reese Kendall.

At Nora's party, Tory had connected dots that I'd missed. The Delicious Memories store had been under construction when Nicole disappeared. Moreover, Tory's investigation had determined that my ex-girlfriend had spent two nights at the motel next door.

As little Neo had asked, "If you were a dead body, where would you be?"

Tory had put in a call to the industrialist, requesting permission to probe beneath the parking lot on his recently acquired property. Not only had he agreed, he'd offered to pay for the procedure in the interest of public relations.

Once Reese and his news team got invested in the search, the result was likely to be a three-ring circus. Still, either they'd find Nicole's remains or the search might move away from this area. I should be so lucky.

"Piper is quite sociable," Jeremiah commented.

I dragged my thoughts back to our subject, which was Piper and her sources of information. "You could have fooled me."

"She has many friends."

Rod retrieved a fuzz ball that had popped behind a water bottle. "She throws parties at your house?"

"No. I was referring to the many phone calls she receives," our companion said.

"From Tory?" I asked.

"I cannot be sure. She removes to her room, and I do not eavesdrop," he said. "Nevertheless, I have the impression there are several different callers."

I had learned to respect his powers of observation. "How can you tell?"

"Her tone of voice changes after she answers," Jeremiah said.

As evenly as possible, I asked, "Does it ever sound as if she's talking to a child?"

"Once, yes."

My heart lurched. *Don't overreact, Eric.* Most likely it had been the child of a friend, or of the cousin who'd directed her my way.

A movement to my left alerted me that my watcher had left her post at the serving line. "More coffee, anyone?" The blocky figure of Yvonne loomed over us as she held out a carafe.

"When did the staff start providing table service?" Rod asked.

"Sir?" She pronounced the single syllable as if it were a freshly sharpened dart, of the poisoned variety.

"I will take some, thank you." Jeremiah held out his cup.

She poured it expertly. "Anyone else?"

Rod and I declined. Our eavesdropper moved off, finally.

As we finished eating, a stir rippled through the large room. It took a moment for me to register that people had, in waves, ceased conversing and consulted their cell phones.

A woman's disembodied voice arose from multiple devices, as if everyone had clicked on the same video. Which, I quickly discovered, they had.

On my phone, I brought up *The Safe Harbor Journal* site, where eager reporter Soraya Montenegro appeared on video. Reese Kendall, who owned both the newspaper and its website, had wasted no time capitalizing on events.

Sunlight emphasized Soraya's star-quality appearance: milk-chocolate skin, dark cloud of hair, sophisticated tan-and-navy suit. Behind her lay the familiar Delicious Memories shop, edged by an empty parking lot. Along the pavement, a man in an orange safety vest and yellow hard hat was pushing what appeared to be a lawn mower.

"Isn't this exciting?" Soraya raised her voice above the hum of traffic from the nearby freeway. About as exciting as watching someone trim hedges, in my opinion, but she was just doing her job. "We're seeing ground-penetrating radar at work! This GPR device sends a high frequency radio signal into the ground and measures how long it takes for it to be reflected back. It's searching for the remains of a woman who went missing nine years ago. A local detective has determined she was staying at the motel next door. Isn't that a horrible thought, that she might have been buried here?"

She glanced off-camera before resuming her narration. "Here's Mr. Reese Kendall, owner of *The Safe Harbor Journal.* He also owns this property and is funding the search."

The camera drew back to include a man who, although not much taller than Soraya in her high heels, dominated by his broad-shouldered presence. In his mid-forties, with dark hair, a tailored suit and sharp blue eyes, he exuded power.

"As soon as I learned of this tragic situation, I knew we had to act," he intoned. "This is the future site of Persia's Perfections, featuring my wife Persia's transformative line of skin-care products. How sad but how rewarding if we could ease the pain of Nicole Blanchard's loved ones by discovering her fate."

"Transformative skin cream?" Rod grumbled. "Some P.R. wonk sure earned her salary with that one."

To me, this situation smacked more of a publicity stunt than a serious search for a murder victim. After a glance at the clock, I stood up. "Patients are waiting."

"For me, also." Jeremiah arose and walked with me.

As we covered the half-block to the medical building, there was no escaping the newscast. Foot traffic in both directions kept phones on speaker.

In snatches, I heard a geophysicist discussing ground-penetrating radar. "The type of soil and water saturation can affect the GPR waves..." A moment later: "Interpreting the data requires experience and...." The next staticky phrase might have been anything. Training? Instinct? Fairy dust?

Standing beside Jeremiah in the lobby, awaiting the elevator, I learned from a tech's yammering cell phone that a common application of the radar was to locate buried utilities such as gas, electrical, water and sewer lines. "But it can identify much more, right?" prompted Soraya's voice.

"GPR has helped uncover ancient ruins, as well as massacre sites from many eras," the geophysicist responded. The tech stared raptly at her little screen.

Under normal conditions, I, too, find archeology and history fascinating. Not today. Silently, I urged the elevator to hurry up but, as usual, it ignored me.

"What about individual burial sites?" the reporter asked breathlessly.

"Yes, it has led to unmarked graves, but you have to dig to confirm the findings," the man continued. "Also, radar is affected by other signals and interference, such as from airplanes, cell phones, power lines and so on. If we aren't successful, I'd suggest bringing in a cadaver dog."

If you aren't successful, maybe there's nothing there. Wishful thinking on my part.

The elevator doors opened and then closed with us inside, cutting off the signal. The tech kept tapping at her phone, as if nagging would unfreeze the video.

On the fourth floor, Jeremiah and I parted ways to our separate offices. At mine, the receptionist tucked something into a drawer. Her phone, no doubt.

My patients were less circumspect and, as the hours wore on, I was subjected to Soraya's intermittent chatter. There were references to bats and dolphins using sound to navigate—echolocation, an expert termed it—and references to the depths to which GPR could penetrate. Depending on the underground material and type of equipment, this ranged from several inches to thousands of feet, although the equipment exploring this lot only extended down a few feet. Deep enough, Soraya speculated, for a killer to have disposed of a body at a construction site.

In her mind and, presumably, in the public's, Nicole's death and burial had become established facts. Even I had trouble recalling that nothing had been verified.

The day ran long, with several post-holiday drop-ins. However, there was plenty of daylight remaining when I left.

As I reached my electric car at its charging station, Jeremiah's long stride brought him abreast. As usual, his identical car was parked next to mine.

"Did you hear?" he asked. "They have found something."

Oh, hell. "What?"

"They are bringing in a team to excavate," he answered.

What lay beneath that parking lot? Construction rubbish, a dead animal, or something more sinister? My phone yielded no immediate enlightenment, other than that an excavation was about to begin. Since it was on private property and privately funded, there was no bureaucratic delay. Unless some advocacy group intervened to demand an environmental impact report—which seemed unlikely—all systems were go.

For me personally, the rational course was to head south toward home. As a rule, I behaved sensibly. But this felt as if someone were drilling into my teeth without an anesthetic.

From the medical center, I turned left and drove north.

Safe Harbor is an old-fashioned California seaside community, with a mix of expensive homes and a few elegant hotels overlooking the small-boat harbor and the beach. Inland lie more modest homes, while the main boulevard is lined with establishments mirroring the life-cycle of the populace: a baby emporium, a toy store, bridal boutiques, a housewares haven, a beauty salon, a flower shop, a funeral home.

A frontage road along the freeway took me to the crowded scene in question. Vehicles lined the street, and the pitted pavement of the Swift & Snug Motel was crammed, despite the Tow-Away Zone placards.

I passed Delicious Memories and, a few blocks farther, eased my car into a curbside gap. A sign warned of Tuesday street-sweeping between 8 a.m. and 5 p.m. It was now nearly 6:30.

Skirting the store on foot, I aimed for the knot of people jockeying for position around the excavation area. Nicole's last resting place, if this was indeed it, was about to be ripped apart amid a quasi-festival atmosphere.

Between the selfie sticks, I glimpsed a couple of workers in safety gear preparing a compressor and a jackhammer. This was going to be noisy. Dusty, too. And they'd need to proceed with care once they broke up the pavement.

People murmured impatiently and shuffled for a better view. Seriously, what did they expect, a dead woman's ghost to leap up and cry for justice?

Maybe for just a little excitement in their humdrum lives. However, as a doctor, I've learned that ordinary lives are far from boring. We all exist in a tumult of dreams, hopes, memories and fears. Lots of fears.

What did I fear at the moment? That they'd locate Nicole, or that she'd be forever lost?

Amid the cluster of watchers, two splashes of bright yellow stood out. Crinkly gray-and-brown hair topped one head, while her companion sported an instantly recognizable multicolored mane. Yvonne and Starla, wearing their cafeteria uniforms, had brought their passion for gossip right to the scene. While Piper had mentioned that Yvonne had no car, I gathered that Starla did. A useful companion.

Yvonne squared her stance as if settling in for the long term. Beside her, Starla smiled toward a man standing nearby. Trent Horner. Present in his capacity as a detective or on his parents' behalf? They must be disturbed by the implication that they'd unwittingly paved over the body of a murder victim.

The throng half-hid Soraya, who'd assumed a position near the not-yet-active jackhammer. Unable to see her clearly, I clicked on my phone's video panel.

"Please describe for our audience exactly what you're doing," she commanded a female hardhat.

"Setting up," came the response.

"How long will that take?"

"As long as it needs to."

The reporter's face scrunched in frustration. How did she

plan to fill the dead air time? I wondered. And got an unexpected answer when she scanned her audience and perked up.

"We've been joined by one of the key players in this drama!" Soraya announced tinnily, over my phone and, faintly, from her actual presence. "Dr. Eric Darcy, the last person to see the missing woman alive, has joined us on site!" The cameraman swung around.

Run! Well, no. Stupidly, I'd worn my white jacket. Did I want to be forever stamped on the public's mind as the idiot racing away with his lab coat flapping?

A strong hand gripped my upper arm. "You shouldn't be here," growled the voice of my friend Keith.

A couple of thoughts collided in my brain. That he was here as a detective observing in case there might be a killer present. That if so, he shouldn't be giving advice to a suspect. And that he might genuinely consider me to be a suspect.

My closest buddy thought I was capable of murder. On the other hand, Keith thought everyone was capable of murder.

"Let's get out of here," I said, grateful for the cluster of bodies preventing Soraya from reaching me.

Keith released my arm. "Pizza, my place." The comforting impression of loyalty evaporated when he nodded to Trent Horner before we both sauntered off.

Still, he'd provided an excuse for a dignified departure. Plus, the rackety roar of a jackhammer cut off any further remarks Soraya might have made.

I'd escaped. But I'd also promised to join Keith at his apartment. And, sadly, I was no longer sure whether I trusted my friend.

CHAPTER SEVEN

Keith's apartment complex was less swanky than Nora's condo development, but still classic Southern California: outdoor entrances, stucco exteriors and ferns tough enough to have survived the age of mammoths. At his unit, the smell that greeted me hinted at unlaundered towels, post-gym sweat and random takeout food.

I hadn't been to his place in the two years since he and Tory broke up. Nobody else had moved in with him, although one girlfriend had tried, leading to a spectacular breakup spat that almost rivaled his split from my sister-in-law.

Discolored rectangles on the walls indicated where Tory had removed artwork, which he'd replaced, inexactly, with posters from national parks. Pride of place in the front room belonged to a gigantic TV, facing an array of seating.

As he marched in, Keith grabbed a beer can and a potato chip bag from the sofa and tossed them in the kitchen trash. From the fridge, he retrieved a box that turned out to contain three-quarters of a pepperoni pizza.

"I don't need to heat this, do I?" he asked

Was this a test of manliness? "Of course not."

After bringing over the box and two cans of beer, he

switched the TV function from his game system to the Internet. The *Journal* site popped up fast, indicating to me that he checked it regularly. Good practice for a police detective.

"I'm surprised you showed up at the dig site." Lodging beside me on the couch, Keith stretched his legs atop the coffee table and pried out the largest slice of pizza. "The situation must be bothering you."

"Yes." I took the second-largest slice.

"Care to elaborate?" He spoke with his mouth full. Not being his mother, I raised no objection.

"No." Cold pizza doesn't exactly fit my definition of a treat. On the other hand, a few days of marinating does intensify the flavors.

"You're in a bad mood."

Because I was usually such a chatterbox? "A man who's falsely accused has a right to be angry."

"You haven't been accused of anything," he said.

Technically true, in the legal sense. "By implication."

"Why is this woman—Dr. Blanchard—so certain you're responsible for whatever happened to her sister?" Keith persisted.

I regretted having spoken freely at Nora's party. Too late to claw it back. "A, because I seem to be the last person who talked to her. B, according to a cousin Piper recently ran into, Nicole claimed she was in danger."

"From you?"

"Not specifically," I said. "Let's be logical. If Nicole believed I posed a threat, surely I'm the last person she'd have contacted."

"People don't always act rationally." Keith popped open his beer.

He hadn't turned on a recorder, as far as I was aware. But for all I knew, his whole apartment might be bugged. *And you're being paranoid.*

On the screen, the din of jackhammers had yielded to the steady thunk-thunk of handheld shovels. Excavation proceeded slowly and cautiously, as if this were an archeological site.

Or a murder scene.

In the foreground, beneath floodlights, Soraya's enthusiasm had assumed a ragged edge. She'd been standing out there for hours, in high heels no less, and it was dinnertime. I almost felt sorry for her.

When a surgeon has a long operation, nurses or other assistants bring sustenance, usually in the form of a sandwich or wrap. They'll hold it up to your mouth, too, as you step away to avoid contaminating the surgical field. Convenient, but not the kind of image a TV personality could afford.

"The crew hired by Safe Harbor businessman Reese Kendall is closing in on what may be a shocking discovery," she told the audience, managing to plug her employer as she recapped the situation. "Has a murdered woman lain beneath this parking lot for years, while cars whiz past on the freeway? Will she finally get justice? And what's her connection to a prominent local doctor who was reputedly her lover?"

"She just told them what the connection is," I snarled.

"You admit you were her lover?" Keith prodded.

"We dated for about a month, a dozen years ago."

"That's all?"

"All of what?"

"You have a talent for getting mixed up in murder investigations," my friend observed. "Maybe you should spend more time with your patients and less time fancying yourself a detective."

This went beyond professional jealousy. "You mean, less time hanging out with Tory," I needled.

Keith's cheekbones, described as "chiseled" in one of

Soraya's articles, sharpened in response. "She moved into your house after you had a break-in, because she claimed you and her father needed protection. What's her excuse now?"

"Free food and rent."

"You should charge her."

"She's family." That wasn't really his issue, though. "You'd rather she moved back in with you."

He studied the TV, although the onscreen activity was literally as dull as dirt. "Things have improved between us. Women always say it's time to move to the next level. Well, a guy can say it, too."

"You might try telling her that," I suggested over my second slice.

"I did. She deflected."

I'm no expert on complicated relationships, and theirs qualified on multiple counts. Acquainted since high school, they hadn't hit it off in the romance department until both were working as police detectives. For over a year, matters had gone well, until Tory caught Keith cheating on her, left this apartment and reinvented herself as a PI.

My bad luck in having my home broken into, plus my possession of a spare bedroom, had provided the excuse for her to invade the premises. Since her father, already living there at my invitation, had been delighted, I'd acquiesced.

During the ensuing turbulence, she'd rejected Keith's apologies, and he'd responded by dating the woman he'd cheated with. Bad idea, resulting in his having to duck the lady's overzealous marital aspirations.

Once Keith conceded that his heart, or bits of it, still belonged to Tory, he and my sister-in-law had begun a delicate tango of drawing closer and then dancing away, the dancing away being mostly on Tory's part.

I'd believed they might finally be in step after he provided emotional support during her recent cancer scare. Apparently not. "She isn't responding according to plan, I take it?"

"How about her and you?" Keith demanded. "Is she your partner in anti-crime again?"

"I assure you, I have nothing to do with Piper Blanchard's case, aside from Tory interrogating me," I said.

"Does that involve sessions alone in a private setting?"

My mouth dropped open. Okay, to admit a bite of pizza, but still. After chewing, I said, "Does this reflect your theory that she had a crush on me in high school?" He'd brought that up previously, to my astonishment. "Get real, Keith."

"I'm never not real."

"Whatever's holding her back with you, it isn't me," I said.

"Good to know."

To cut off this fruitless discussion, I headed for the bathroom, passing through a hall that sported several large framed photos. My gaze skimmed over a shot of Keith and the rest of our high school football team, powder-blue uniforms emblazoned with orange-and-white letters. In another picture, Keith posed with his two husky brothers and their parents in front of a Christmas tree.

His dad had been police chief in a nearby city. After his retirement, he and Keith's mom had moved to Oregon to be near their older sons, both successful businessmen with wives and kids. Although Keith flew up there for Christmas, he'd never been as close to his brothers, growing up, as he had been to me.

A third image stopped me cold. It was my wedding photo, a duplicate of one hanging in my house. A younger me, tuxedo-clad, towered above my petite, black-haired bride, whose luminous face seemed to stand out in three dimensions. On my other side stood a slimmer version of Keith, next to the short figure of my brother-in-law, Barry. Beside Lydia, Tory gripped her bouquet as if prepared to wrestle it into submission. Lydia's friend Shana completed the group with the unruffled air of an experienced bridesmaid.

Had someone been murdering Nicole while the bunch of us stood there, oblivious? Or had she been fleeing the city, her fears and secrets locked inside? I must have wiped our brief conversation from memory almost immediately, because I didn't recall thinking of her a single time that day.

My feelings kept tangling with the notion that she might have borne my child. Should I mention it to Keith? But he would no doubt relay it to his colleagues, which was likely to add to my supposed motives for disposing of her.

What if I had a son or daughter? Where? Growing up how? A painfully familiar grip in the chest stayed with me for the next few minutes.

When I returned to the living room, Soraya was interviewing Piper onscreen. "What brought you to Safe Harbor nine years after your sister disappeared?"

"I came across new information." Piper raised a hand to shield her eyes from the floodlights.

"You believe her body is buried where those workers are digging?" Soraya extended the microphone.

"If she was murdered, she might be here." In the harsh lighting, Piper's face had a ghostly pallor.

"How do you feel about that?"

"Scared. Anxious. How would *you* feel?"

Soraya pressed on. "You must want answers."

"Damn straight."

"What do you know about her relationship to Dr. Eric Darcy?"

Here we go again, damn it.

"He's admitted talking to her the last night she was seen." Piper's face tightened as she glanced toward the diggers.

"Did they have a turbulent relationship? Was it ongoing?"

"I think he's the reason she dropped out of medical school."

"What?" I popped up from the couch. "That was several months later. Her mother had cancer."

On the TV, Soraya pressed, "Could you elaborate on that?"

"Not really."

I resumed my seat and reached for the pizza box. Empty.

"You snooze, you lose," Keith said.

"Why didn't you stick around the crime scene, if it is one?" I prodded him.

"I can't be involved in this," my friend said. "Thanks to you, I'm a potential witness."

"Thanks to my stupidity in asking you to be my best man," I growled. "And what exactly did you witness?"

"You, acting like a besotted bridegroom, that evening and the next morning."

I thought of the photo in the hall. It would take a sociopath to pose placidly with his bridal party after ending a woman's life, but you can't help what people believe. I've seen the media whip up hysteria too often to trust in the public's good judgment.

"What gripes me, besides having my name dragged through the mud, is that if Nicole was murdered, it's a waste of time focusing on me," I said. "Someone else did it."

"Any idea who had a motive?" A serious note darkened Keith's tone.

Honestly, I'd been too busy hoping Nicole was safe to spend much energy thinking about that. Now that he'd brought it up, though... "If she was in danger, my guess is it's from someone in Alaska. Maybe she was dating a possessive guy. Or she owed debts or got into drugs. Or she witnessed a crime."

"Why contact you?"

"To borrow money," I speculated. "She didn't ask for any.

But she might have intended to."

"And while she was here, she happened to run into some evil dude purely by chance?"

"You're assuming she's dead. But if she is, whoever she was fleeing might have tracked her."

At a stir on the video, our conversation broke off. Behind the two women, the hardhats had ceased their labors and one of them was signaling. I glimpsed Tory moving toward him from the side.

"They've found something!" Soraya's eyes widened at the unseen camera operator. "Can you get a closer view?"

"What is it?" Piper sounded shaky. "Tory! What is it?"

"Isn't that your private investigator?" Soraya asked. "Ms. Golden, please enlighten us."

The view widened to include my sister-in-law's tall figure. Keith leaned forward on the couch. "She should stay out of it."

Someone must have spoken to Soraya from off-camera, because she blared out a stunning declaration. "Bones! There are bones in that hole!"

Stunned, Piper turned to look, although I doubted she could see anything from where she stood. I shared her distress. *Please don't let that be Nicole.*

While Trent Horner had never been my favorite police detective, I experienced a surge of gratitude when he intruded. "This is now a potential crime scene. Everyone, please step back."

"How will you determine whether those are the remains of Nicole Blanchard?" Soraya demanded.

"We just notified the coroner's office," Trent said. "If the bones prove to be human, they'll attempt to make the identification. Everyone, please clear the area."

"My sister!" Ignoring him, Piper started forward.

"You shouldn't see this." Tory held out a restraining arm,

but she was too far away to stop the onrushing woman. At the trench, Piper dropped to her knees and shined her phone's light into the depths.

"Dr. Blanchard, I have to ask you to move away." That was Trent, shaking his head.

"No!" Piper's shriek shivered through me. "That hair clip! I gave it to her for Sweet Sixteen."

I went cold.

"Are you sure?" Tory asked.

"I made it myself. There can't be another one like it."

Nicole hadn't moved on, hadn't assumed another identity, hadn't gone into hiding. She'd died here in Safe Harbor, and you don't bury yourself in a construction site after overdosing or committing suicide.

She'd reached out to me, and I'd turned her away. Then someone had killed her.

CHAPTER EIGHT

Three days later, after work on Friday, Jeremiah joined me as I exited through the office building's lobby, where I got the sense he'd been lingering. Until recently, his presence would have annoyed me, but not today. Concern about this case had brought us into alignment.

The week had been disturbing in multiple respects. I might say hellish, except that I'd experienced worse after my wife's death. This time, the pain resulted from the death of a woman who'd been relegated to the distant recesses of memory until her ghost burst forth to haunt me.

After dropping by the station at the request of Leo Franco, I'd elaborated on what I'd told the sergeant at the Labor Day party, and endured hours of overlapping questions by him and Trent Horner intended to jog my memory, or to trip me up if I were lying. I hoped they realized I wasn't.

Frankly, I didn't see how any normal person could stick to an invented story in the face of such intense and complex probing. As it was, they'd dredged up a few minor inconsistencies, as memories surfaced and details proved slightly inaccurate. Exactly what time had I arrived home the night Nicole called? How long had the conversation lasted?

Who else had I spoken to that evening? Yet, in the end, nothing of substance emerged, in my opinion.

Other witnesses also went under the knife, in the metaphoric sense. They included Tory, of course, who drew detectives' attention both as the investigator who'd located the remains and as a witness to my behavior before and after the presumed homicide. Never a cheerful spirit, she stomped around our house muttering dourly after being interviewed. I gathered she hated having the case removed from her control, and also that her client was being less than cooperative about Tory's offers of further assistance.

Piper had been so distraught that she'd stopped seeing patients, forcing Chuck and other doctors to fill in. Jeremiah in particular had taken over many surgeries and deliveries.

If the police learned anything significant from Piper, it hadn't made the local news. That didn't stop Soraya from peppering her videos and articles with questions. Had Nicole been fleeing a homicidal boyfriend—or girlfriend—in Juneau? Why had Nicole traveled to Safe Harbor and contacted me? Had she demanded money?

There was even, out of the blue, a question about whether she'd left behind any children, a point Soraya claimed had been suggested by an unnamed "interested member of the public." I presumed that was Piper.

Her toying with the possibility that Nicole and I had had a child was a cruel way to try to manipulate me into what, a confession? Despite Tory's previous comment that Piper believed I'd killed her sister and therefore considered me fair game, any reasonable person would cough up the truth about this maybe offspring and let the police apply the screws. I'd have preferred that to this uncertainty.

"The coroner's office should have released the cause of death by today," Jeremiah commented en route to the parking garage. He had to temper his long stride to match mine.

"The only surprise would be if Nicole *wasn't* murdered," I said grimly.

"I am reluctant to return home," he continued. "I presume they will inform Piper before any public announcement, and there is no telling how she will react. I am not comfortable with emotional displays."

"She's been freaking out?" Since the electric recharging stations on the garage's lower level had been occupied, I'd parked on the second floor. We climbed the stairs with Jeremiah a step below me, tall enough that our heads were almost level.

"Piper has a tendency toward dramatics," he said, rather close to my ear.

"For example?" Not that I couldn't have supplied instances from my own observation, but those had been directed at me.

"There have been outbursts of sobbing. Once, she fled to her room and slammed the door," he said. "I believe custom requires me to offer comfort, but when I recommended she consult the hospital psychologist, she termed me an insensitive clod."

"Is that when she ran to her room and slammed the door?" I asked as we arrived at Level Two.

"Yes."

I sympathized with this reluctant landlord, sucked into a maelstrom he was ill-prepared to handle. I also felt restless and tired of replaying speculations in my head.

"Why don't you come to my house for dinner?" I startled myself by asking. "There are plenty of leftovers."

"I would like that," he responded solemnly. "Thank you."

"Good. You know the address?"

"I have not forgotten."

During my residency at UC Irvine, my dad and I had hosted

several gatherings for my colleagues, which had included Jeremiah. Later, when I feared he was stalking Lydia, I'd watched for him outside, in vain. As I'd later come to understand, he'd have gained nothing by such surveillance, since his goal had been to duplicate my public behavior.

"I will see you." He strode off.

At my house, the presence of the brown sedan with the "Cancer Cures Smoking" bumper sticker signaled that my cleaning team remained on the premises. Morris had a catering job that night, I recalled, and Tory's space in the garage was empty.

Inside, Keely and Starla lugged their equipment past me toward the utility room. Once again, I'd arrived as they finished.

"Have you been keeping up with the news?" Starla burbled. "That reporter interviewed Trent! Isn't it exciting?"

From what I'd glimpsed of the latest video, the segment had consisted of Soraya waylaying the detective outside the police department and him providing the standard "it's under investigation." He'd referred all questions to the public information officer.

"The P.I.O.'s on leave," the reporter had countered.

Trent had hesitated only a blink before responding, "Then call the chief's office."

Some interview.

"Sorry, Doctor," Keely told me. "I swear, we haven't been standing around watching the news."

"I never thought you had," I assured her.

Keely nodded. "We'll be off, then."

But, as if unable to walk and talk simultaneously, Starla planted herself in my path. The unpleasant scent of cigarette smoke drifted from her. "Trent's my boyfriend."

"You met at the Suncrest Saloon?" I guessed.

"Sure did!" She beamed at me. "Thanks for recommending it."

"One date doesn't qualify him as your boyfriend," Keely said.

Starla giggled. "I almost wish I was a witness so he'd grill me!" A sobering thought must have stumbled into her mind, because she added, "Except if I was a witness, he couldn't go out with me, could he?"

The doorbell rang. "That's Dr. Schwartz," I said. "Thanks, both of you."

"Always a pleasure to work in such a beautiful home." A smile cracked Keely's granite face.

"But if you ever need a decorator..." Her companion left the sentence unfinished as Keely poked her in the ribs.

When Jeremiah entered, he greeted the two ladies with cool politeness. After their departure, he followed my lead in helping himself to leftovers, declining a beer in favor of orange juice.

We carried our plates to the greenhouse nook, with its multi-paned windows and clouded-glass chandelier. Although it has a lovely view overlooking my mother's rose garden, I'm usually too lazy to move a few dozen feet farther than the kitchen table. However, I was drawn by the medium-size screen tucked into one corner, which—anticipating an announcement from the coroner's office—I clicked on.

At the *Journal* site, the video rectangle remained dark. My eye went instead to that morning's print story about the case, featuring a photo of Nicole. She was laughing, long golden hair blowing around her shoulders, a slight sideways narrowing of the eyes warning that unpredictable behavior lay ahead.

Was Soraya taking a break after a week of pounding the story like a piñata? More likely, she was working on tomorrow's account. Or busy harassing the chief's office about the lack of a P.I.O.

I switched between a couple of Los Angeles news stations, but they displayed only the customary car chases and brush fires. I switched off the set.

Taking a break from my pita sandwich, I said, "I'd appreciate it if you would tell me more about Piper. Has she shared anything fresh about Nicole?"

"She has not confided in me," Jeremiah replied. "Her behavior is not logical, unless there are facts of which we are unaware."

"I'm sure there are," I said. "I was hoping she'd slipped and revealed information to you."

He dabbed his mouth with his napkin before saying, "She has not. I am also dubious that she has disclosed everything to the police."

As always, I put stock in his powers of observation. "Why do you think that?"

"She has been ducking their requests for a more in-depth interview. She screens her calls in my presence."

"They've left messages?"

"Yes, several, which she has ignored."

Was that due to her distress, or a more sinister motive? I wondered. What could she be hiding? Was she protecting someone? "Is she still having hushed phone conversations?"

"Yes." After a pause, he said, "I still have not discerned the identities of her friends."

"She could be getting support from people back home," I speculated.

"She went out last night for more than an hour," Jeremiah said. "Since she is not seeing patients or delivering babies, I presume she met with someone."

"Then he or she must be staying in the area." What if this was the killer? Maybe he and Piper were scheming to shift the blame onto me, or he was threatening her. If they'd met at a bar or restaurant, they might have been captured on camera. "Have you spotted any receipts or takeout sacks lying around?"

"Only a carton of leftovers from the hospital cafeteria," Jeremiah replied. "I doubt they tasted as good as this."

I thanked him on Morris's behalf. We ate in silence for a while as I mulled what I knew, or thought I knew.

"Piper claimed she ran into a cousin who had information about Nicole," I recalled. "Do you suppose that's who she's meeting?" Perhaps that cousin had followed her here, or someone else had, someone with an ulterior motive.

Like covering up a murder.

"On further reflection, there is another matter of interest." Jeremiah set down his fork. "Piper explained that one of her reasons for leaving Alaska was the recent breakup of a relationship. She was dating a pilot who turned out to have that cliché, a girl in every port."

"Or airport."

"I do not believe they were literally waiting on the tarmac." He ducked his head. "You spoke figuratively."

"Still, you've raised a valuable point," I said. "Whoever she's talking to might not be staying here. A pilot could easily fly in and out." John Wayne Airport lay only a few miles away.

Jeremiah considered this. "If she has resumed a relationship with such a faithless man, she is foolish."

"She's certainly emotionally fragile. But, in fairness, almost anyone would be off-center after the discovery of her sister's remains," I conceded.

"Perhaps Piper suffers from a psychological disorder," he said. "Schizophrenia is not the only type of mental illness and hallucinations are not the only type of delusions."

"That opens a wide range of possibilities," I agreed.

The inner door from the garage smacked shut. It didn't

exactly slam, but this was Tory's way of indicating her mood was irritable.

Into the kitchen she trudged, thudding her laptop onto the table. No surprise that she had to keep replacing her equipment.

Across the dozen or so feet separating us, she cast a glare in my direction. The sight of Jeremiah must have cut short whatever she had been about to say, so she just stood there, scowling.

"What's going on?" I asked.

"You haven't heard?"

I shook my head.

"Seriously?"

"Seriously and every other way."

Several seconds ticked by.

"Is this your customary manner of communicating with your sister-in-law?" Jeremiah inquired.

"This is my sister-in-law's customary manner of acting like a dick," I said.

He frowned. "That is how detectives behave?"

"Not that kind of dick. The obnoxious kind."

His gaze traveled between us. I empathized with the man's failure to grasp the undertones, because my sister-in-law's attitude was irrational.

Tory got tired of waiting for a response. "The coroner released his report."

"And?"

"Strangulation," she said. "There was a fracture of the hy-something bone."

"Hyoid." A stab of pain in my rib cage cut off further words. Here it was, hard and final, the ugly fact that an attacker had squeezed the life out of Nicole.

Subconsciously, I'd been hoping she'd simply fallen during

a fight and struck her head, or been accidentally hit by a car. Far-fetched scenarios, but in such a case death might have caught her suddenly, without time for fear.

Strangulation meant she'd suffered. That she'd died terrified and helpless. That she'd known, at least for a moment, what was happening.

"You are pale, Eric," Jeremiah observed. "You must be experiencing a surge of stress hormones. Do you feel light-headed or queasy?"

"No, but thanks."

"If he has any decency, he feels like a jerk." Tory rested her elbows on the counter, oblivious to the spilled sauce. "There's more."

"More?" My voice echoed from a cavern in my head.

"What delayed the report, it seems, was certain questions that had been raised." She spoke stiffly. "The coroner's office has an anthropologist on staff. And he confirmed what we suspected, Eric."

"What's that?"

"Nicole Blanchard had given birth."

CHAPTER NINE

Tory's words racketed through my brain. Nicole had had a baby.

My longed-for fatherhood had been warped and denied to me, and my protection and love had been denied to a child that might have been mine. Nicole hadn't even allowed me to offer support. Now the truth was being hurled at me in the worst way imaginable, as the result of violence and in public, exposing me to blame as well as grief.

As I struggled to regularize my breathing, I stared out at the rose garden, its pops of reds and pinks fragmented by the window segments. There my mother had sought peace from the agony of cancer and, before that, from another kind of pain.

Annette Darcy had loved being a mom, and had told me she'd dreamed as a young girl of having four children. There'd been infertility problems, never shared with me in any detail. I recalled a tearful episode when I was a child, quickly hidden away behind a closed door, that I presumed had been a miscarriage. Although I hadn't consciously drawn on her sorrow when I chose my specialty, it had provided a special empathy with patients.

Now I grasped at a visceral level some of the hollowness,

the rage, and the grief Mom must have felt. I'd heard insensitive clods dismiss the suffering of infertile women and those who miscarried, as if you couldn't be devastated by the loss of a child you'd never held in your arms. Like hell you couldn't.

"When did this happen?" Thank goodness Jeremiah remained able to pose sensible questions. "Was it shortly before her death, or years earlier?"

"They couldn't tell the time frame, only that she'd had a child." Tory shoved a strand of chestnut hair behind her ear.

My companion nodded. "The birth could have occurred at any point in her life after puberty."

Finally, I was able to breathe. Nicole might have become a mother before she met me, or during the ensuing three years prior to her death. "Do they have any idea where the child is?"

"I'm sure they're searching birth records in Juneau." Tory said. "Come clean, Eric. Whatever you're covering up, out with it."

"What a pile of crap!" Fury fired me to my feet. "Stop assuming I'm guilty."

"I make no assumptions."

"Liar!"

Tory's mouth opened as if to challenge me. Did she honestly think I'd walked down the aisle with her sister, smiled and danced and hugged people, right after I'd strangled a woman? More than that, a woman who, according to this bizarre scenario, had just informed me that I had a child?

My lifelong habit of restraint shattered. "There's not one damn bit of evidence against me because I didn't do anything," I roared. "If you're gullible enough to buy into your client's paranoia, that says far more about your character than you appear to have learned about mine in the past couple of decades. If you think I murdered Nicole, you aren't smart enough to be a detective."

"I didn't mean that." Tory frowned. "What did I say, exactly?"

I was too furious to answer. Almost too furious to breathe.

"You ordered him to come clean," Jeremiah said. "You claimed he was engaging in a cover-up. This indicates to me that you believe him to have committed a serious breach of ethics or the law."

My sister-in-law spread her hands apologetically. "I didn't mean that, Eric. I know you wouldn't reject your child or hurt a woman. I doubt you've ever harmed anybody in your life."

"Been tempted." I didn't need to specify.

"I'm sorry." Tory met my gaze straight on. "The circumstances of this case have me rattled."

"The discovery that I had an affair or that someone murdered Nicole?"

"Both." Her shoulders slumped. "You were Lydia's knight in shining armor. Like Piper said, the golden boy."

"And you're shocked that I'm just an ordinary person, and therefore deserve your contempt?" I wasn't about to let her off.

"You going to hold this against me?" she asked. "Do I need to move out?"

I nearly said yes. But knee-jerk reactions can have long-term, unpleasant consequences.

While Tory is far from the easiest person to be around, she's as much a victim of her bad temper as anyone. I've often wondered if she regretted her impulsive decision to quit the police department after her breakup with Keith. The attitude of their colleagues, many of whom sympathized with the cheater, had infuriated her.

As a result, she'd lost her once-loved career, her steady income with generous benefits, and a lot of buddies. She'd also landed on my curb, too proud to admit she was seeking shelter.

Now she was proposing that I kick her to the curb, literally. Was that really what I wanted? "Let's not be hasty," I muttered. "Have dinner."

Jeremiah arose. "Thank you for the repast, Eric. I will depart and hope my housemate is not experiencing a meltdown."

"She's not answering her phone, whatever that indicates," Tory advised.

"It is beyond my scope to guess what her actions signify." Courteously, he bid her farewell.

After Jeremiah left, I cut myself a slice of pie and watched my sister-in-law plow through her meal. Should I accept her offer to move? It would be painful for Morris, but satisfying to Keith. Not that she'd necessarily rejoin him. In fact, that seemed highly unlikely.

I tried to recall what life had been like before she moved in here. Quieter, calmer. Duller. Besides, that wasn't the point. For whatever weird reason, or no reason at all, I loved Lydia's feisty, pain-in-the-neck younger sister and preferred to keep an eye on her.

She was definitely a work in progress. Well, aren't we all?

Her plate empty, Tory set down her fork. "I've been debating why I'm so upset about this situation. On a personal level, I mean."

"Drawn any conclusion?"

The light from the small chandelier picked out gold flecks in her green eyes. "It's the sister thing. I instinctively identify with Piper. If I'd lost Lydia like this, if I was convinced a particular man caused her death, I'd have turned over a lot more than a stretch of pavement to get..."

"Revenge?" I filled in.

"Justice. That's the cliché, right?"

"Accusing the wrong person isn't justice," I said. "Ignoring evidence isn't justice."

"Why do you say she's ignoring evidence?"

Examples sprang to mind. "She dodges tough questions, like whether her sister had a baby, which we can now see was true. Or about this cousin she supposedly ran into, who implied I was dangerous. And, according to Jeremiah, she goes out and meets with someone, yet she's new in town and hasn't introduced him to any friends."

"Good points." Tory rested her elbows on the table. The sauce on them had dried from earlier, I observed. "What else?"

I searched my memory. "She lied about spreading gossip at the hospital. Tried to blame it on a cafeteria lady, who I'll concede is a rude snoop, but I don't believe Piper shared that much personal stuff with a stranger."

She mulled over my observations. "It's surprising how helpful you can be in reviewing a case."

"This is news to you?" I didn't hesitate to employ sarcasm. Directed toward most people, it would strike me as offensive. In my sister-in-law's case, I considered it the most effective way to cut through her bull. "After the murders and missing persons we've looked into? Not to mention that I'm a trained observer and diagnostician."

"Do you really believe I'm not smart enough to be a detective?" Hard to tell whether she felt hurt. More likely, just sorting me out.

"You do occasionally let your emotions trip you up."

"You play hunches," she reminded me. "Isn't that the same thing?"

"My hunches are reasonable interpretations of data."

"When a woman does it, she's acting on emotion," Tory said. "When a guy does it, he's making a—oh, never mind."

I smiled. "Friends again?"

"Never stopped."

Chimes intruded. Had Jeremiah forgotten something?

"Stay." Tory headed across the great room.

The door clicked open. "He's here, isn't he?" demanded a shrill voice I recognized with dismay.

"He lives here," Tory said evenly. "Piper, this isn't appropriate."

"Don't tell me what's appropriate!" Into view stomped the doctor's rapier-thin figure, long pale hair askew, a sheet of paper clutched in one hand. "This! This!" She waved it at me.

"What's that?"

"As if you didn't write it!"

Striding alongside her, Tory plucked the paper from her grasp and read aloud: "Where's my daughter? Tell me or else!!" She checked the flip side, which I could already see was blank, then reexamined the block printing. "'Daughter' is spelled d-a-w-t-e-r."

I wasn't sure what that indicated to her. That a physician couldn't have written it? But we aren't all great spellers.

"On my windshield. At my home!" Piper rapped out each word like a drumbeat.

"You're receiving threats?" *Obviously, Eric.* Keeping my voice steady, I asked, "For how long?"

"Stop it!" She appeared on the verge of tears. "You won't get away with this."

"It's not signed and that doesn't look like Eric's writing," Tory noted. "Did you show it to the police? And quit handling it. You'll mess up the prints."

"He's too smart to leave prints. But people have heard him bragging that he'll shut me up like he did my sister!"

There was no limit to her outrageous accusations. "Who claims they heard me? Where and when?"

Ignoring my questions, Piper faced Tory, who was sliding the note into a clear plastic bag. "It's your job to protect me. You should have found out what he knows by now and got him arrested so we'd be safe."

We. As if she were protecting someone else, too—a child? Or she might be delusional, as Jeremiah had suggested. I hadn't ruled out alcoholism, either, especially in view of Nicole's excessive drinking. Not all relatives share a tendency toward alcoholism, but it does run in families.

"You hired me to dig into facts, not to frame Eric," Tory said.

"And you've accomplished zilch!"

"I located your sister's body."

"Anyone could have done that! Why do you suppose I hired a PI who lives with him?"

My sister-in-law's ears reddened. "So I could manipulate him, as opposed to learning the truth?"

"Here's the truth!" Piper fired back. "You and the cops in this town are corrupt. You protect your own, that's what you do."

They stood half a dozen feet apart, Tory looming over the smaller woman. "I'll make allowances for your rudeness because I presume someone from the coroner's office met with you today about the cause of death. It must have been a shock."

I was on my feet now, too. "Not that much of a shock. She was aware that Nicole had had a baby. Where is she, Piper? I didn't write that message but clearly someone's threatening you and a child who might be mine. Maybe they're using you to try to get to him or her. Would you stop and think for a change?"

Piper clasped her hands together, her gaze shifting between Tory and me. "You're right about one thing. I didn't think. Just like Nicole, I went flying straight at you. And here I am, in danger. I should have listened!"

"To whom?" I demanded. "Who is this person who claims to have heard me, who's feeding you lies?"

Once again ignoring me, she zeroed in on Tory. "You're the

person lying to me, you and your monster of a brother-in-law. What're you, in love with him? What a poor excuse for a detective you are! You're fired. And incompetent! Before I'm done, I'll get your license pulled."

Tory spoke through a clenched jaw. "Just tell the police everything, including where the kid is."

"Trust them? Like they've done such a great job so far," Piper cried out.

Someone had to break through her hysteria. "If I have a child, I want to take care of her, not hurt her. The threat indicates it's a girl. Is that true? If it is, somebody knows something about her. Who is it?"

The woman glared at me with pure hatred. "You can't intimidate me. I'll get a court order against you for harassment."

I refused to tolerate bullying. "Who's harassing whom? You came to my house, not the other way around."

"You're the one issuing threats!" Piper hurled, as if she hadn't just threatened Tory with having her license revoked and me with a court order.

Darting forward, she snatched the plastic sleeve from Tory, and fled. Too late, I wished we'd copied the damn message.

After the front door thumped shut, Tory and I stood processing the confrontation. I was shaking inside. Maybe outside, too.

"That must be why she's fixated on blaming you." Tory waved in the direction of Piper's departure. "Someone's threatening her."

"And doing their best to put the blame on me. Why—to manipulate me into revealing my alleged secrets?"

"As you indicated, they might assume you have inside information." For a change, Tory was following along instead of arguing.

"About Nicole's baby." That raised a disquieting possibility. "Maybe it's always been about this child. Nicole might have been strangled in a botched attempt to force out the location."

"If that's true, whoever killed her obviously didn't get his hands on the kid," Tory assured me. "Otherwise, why keep pushing Piper, and you?"

"That means the child is still alive." But where? In whose care? "There's only one person who would want a child this badly. The father. The real father."

"Or someone who assumes he's the real father." Tory shook her head. "But where's he been for the past nine years? And where's the child been?"

I wondered if the police were asking these questions. Maybe, but would they ask them soon enough to prevent another tragedy? Piper's fixation on me might be blinding her to the real peril.

"Since she fired you, she's no longer your client," I said. "I'd like to hire you."

"To do what?"

"Track clues that aren't a high priority for the police. For starters, I'm sure they view me as a suspect, and that'll take them nowhere." I was breathing normally again, almost. "What about the cousin Piper claims she ran into, who told her Nicole planned to fly down here?"

Tory wandered to the table. "You think this so-called cousin might be the father? But that's kind of weird. I mean, incestuous and all."

"Maybe he's a distant cousin. Anyway, I seem to recall that Piper originally indicated the cousin was a woman." No sense worrying about that. "The whole cousin business was probably a lie. Piper takes unreliability to extremes."

"She's so convinced of your guilt that she ignores any indications to the contrary." Tory collected our empty plates.

"And paranoid about you being buddies with a cop."

"I'm guessing she knows things that could help identify the killer, if she'd only share them." Whoever he was, he'd manipulated her into serving as his more-or-less willing accomplice in clouding the picture. "I'll write a check for your retainer right now."

Tory wrinkled her nose. "Just because she fired me, that doesn't mean I don't owe her any loyalty."

"What about her trying to have your PI license revoked?"

"She won't."

Okay, probably not. "I wonder if it's ever occurred to her that her life might be in danger," I said.

"It's certainly occurred to me. Along with the fact that, if she's killed, you'll be person of interest number one." My sister-in-law began stowing leftovers from the counter. "Stay away from her. No more confrontations, no visits to Jeremiah's house, no checking her car for notes on the windshield."

As if I'd do such a stupid thing. Well, okay, maybe I'd have dropped by Jeremiah's place. "Fine."

"Answer's still no," Tory said. "You're free to hire someone else, of course. I could name several qualified candidates, not necessarily from my firm."

"No, thanks." The prospect of spilling this mess into a stranger's lap was massively unappealing. "That's your notion of helping me?"

She shrugged. "I'll tell the police about Piper's visit tonight and the message on her windshield. Beyond that, it's their case, and I'm out of it."

I wished I were out of it, too. Instead, I had to wait for my unknown enemy to act again.

And next time, he might do more than leave an ugly note.

CHAPTER TEN

Despite the serious issues weighing on my mind, my biggest frustration Saturday morning was being unable to find my sports watch. I normally used it in the exercise room, then returned it to my bureau drawer in the bedroom. When I decided to enjoy the crisp weather by going for a run, I looked forward to its ridiculously complex ability to track everything from my heart rate to my music playlist.

Not in the drawer. Not in the exercise room. Not in the bathroom. No response when I tried to locate it electronically.

My wrist felt denuded as I set out. As I ran, the sea breeze filled my lungs and, between the tall houses on the bluff side of my street, I glimpsed the harbor far below. Sunlight glinted off the blue surface dotted by colorful sails. Low and steady, the rumble of surf blended with the murmur of traffic from distant roads.

How foolish to raise a mental fuss over a device that I'd managed without quite happily for most of my thirty-seven years. Lacking musical accompaniment, I relished the catlike mewing of gulls and the occasional bark of a fenced-in pooch.

Aside from a scattering of dog-walkers and other joggers, I had the sidewalk to myself. Since I don't live near Jeremiah, there was little risk of running into Piper. Tory had been correct about the wisdom of avoiding her.

In today's newspaper, Soraya had offered no revelations I hadn't already heard, just the coroner's report on Nicole's cause of death and the indications of a previous birth. She provided a vague explanation of how this was determined, due to stress scars where the uterine support ligaments attach to the pelvic bone.

The article also cited an unnamed spokesman for the department, who stated that detectives were checking for any similar unsolved murders or disappearances in the area, and that they were coordinating their investigation with police in Juneau, where Nicole had been reported missing.

For once, I had more information than the reporter, since Piper had essentially confirmed to me that the baby was a girl. And she must have been born roughly twelve years ago, since Piper apparently believed the child was mine,.

Dwelling too deeply on that possibility tore at my heart. Even worse was the fear that my daughter might have come to harm.

Where was she? If someone was seeking her, who was it?

Logically, for him to be the father, the killer must have slept with Nicole in Boston or immediately after her return to Alaska. He had also tracked her to Safe Harbor, where he'd strangled her. And he'd left a threat on Piper's windshield, which meant he was here now.

With a jolt, I realized I knew one man who more or less fit those particulars. However, he was the last person I believed capable of cold-blooded murder, or any kind of murder.

Jeremiah.

One could speculate that, in the grip of a delusion, he might slay someone he believed posed an immediate danger to him or someone close to him. But the steps this murderer had taken, from strangling Nicole and burying her in a construction site, to planting messages on Piper's car, displayed an obsessive, manipulative, sociopathic mind unlike my friend's.

Nevertheless, to view the situation as an investigator might, I reviewed how Piper had come to live in Jeremiah's house. Had he maneuvered her in some way?

I thought back to that night two weeks earlier when he'd asked me to verify that she wasn't a delusion. She'd stated in my presence that her nurse had told her about the available room. Okay, a master puppeteer could presumably have engineered the whole situation, but to me that lacked plausibility. Whether or not the police considered Jeremiah a person of interest, I didn't.

That reminded me of the suspicion that the killer was fixated on the child. That might be someone from Boston, but more likely a man who'd entered Nicole's life in Alaska.

I hoped the police were thinking along the same lines. If they identified a boyfriend who'd since moved to Safe Harbor, they could nail him.

Tangled in speculations, I jogged down a footpath that sloped between streets. I paid little attention to my surroundings until the pungent scent of rotting vegetation slapped my senses.

I'd reached Pelican Lane, which ran along a saltwater marsh that marked the eastern limits of town. Only a single house remained of those that had once lined the dead-end street, the others having been acquired by private interests who'd torn them down to create a bird sanctuary. The large stucco home with a wide porch and trellised roses stood out in landscaped solitude.

Several cars lined the street and the gravel driveway. A brown sedan bore the familiar "Cancer Cures Smoking" bumper sticker.

This was the residence where Keely rented a room. Should I ring the bell to ask if she'd seen my watch? She might have tucked it somewhere while dusting yesterday. On the other hand, I hated to disturb the occupants, since the newspaper still lay in the driveway, which indicated they might be sleeping.

As I stood weighing my next move, the front door opened. With her usual fastidiousness, Keely had donned a blouse and slacks rather than shuffling out in her bathrobe.

The heavyset nurse acknowledged my presence with a puzzled nod. Since it would be awkward to simply trot off, I jogged in place as she approached.

"Doctor?" Keely bent from the knees to scoop up the paper.

"I misplaced my sports watch," I said. "I wondered if you saw it lying around yesterday."

She narrowed her eyes as if viewing my rooms on a screen. "No. You don't usually leave that out, do you?"

"I keep it in a bureau drawer."

"Starla cleaned the master bedroom." She scowled. "I'll search her things. If she stole from you, I'll kick her butt clear to Utah."

I hadn't meant to imply theft. "It may have fallen behind a piece of furniture. Or I put it in the wrong place."

"I'll search anyway," Keely said.

"Please don't imply I accused her of anything."

"I know the meaning of discretion, doctor."

"Of course."

Onto the block hummed a silver short-bed pickup. It swung around and glided to the curb.

Out hopped Starla, her pink-and-blue hair mussed. "Thanks, sweetie." She waggled her fingers at the man behind the wheel.

Short blond hair, pale eyes, an embarrassed grin. "More than welcome." With a wave to Keely and me, Detective Trent

Horner drove away.

"Hi, Dr. Darcy." Starla beamed. "What brings you to our doorstep?"

Might as well be straightforward. "Since I was passing, I thought I'd ask if you or Keely spotted my sports watch while you were cleaning. Black band, large face."

"Expensive?" she asked.

That seemed an odd question. "Not excessively."

"Those things hold personal information, don't they?" Starla asked. "I mean, like, you could record stuff on them, right?"

Odder and odder. "My heart rate and jogging route." Since it also received updates to my personal calendar and other data, it was password protected.

"You seem awful interested in how valuable it is," Keely said sternly. "Did you take it?"

"Just curious. Gotta go clean up. I'm meeting friends." With a wink, Starla half-skipped up the walkway.

"She's a nosy thing. I apologize," the older woman said.

"It's not your fault." I didn't hold her responsible for the imperfections of a relative. But the younger woman's responses did strike me as evasive.

Was Starla spying for Trent? Perhaps only in her imagination. While I wasn't sure about the admissibility of evidence accessed via theft, I was pretty sure a cop who trafficked in stolen valuables could land in trouble.

I took out my phone, which accompanies me everywhere, since I have to be available in emergencies. "I'd better deactivate the watch as a precaution. I'm pretty sure I can do it remotely." While that would prove a hassle if the watch turned up safe and sound, Starla's questions had made me uncomfortable. Passwords aren't perfect.

"Good luck. I'll advise you if I find it." Keely toted the paper inside.

Within minutes, I'd shut off the watch via my phone, and picked up a text from Labor and Delivery. The OB on duty needed help with a couple of C-sections.

I replied that I'd be there within an hour. Barely time to finish my run and take a quick shower.

Several surgeries and a couple of deliveries later, I dropped into the doctors' lounge. The vending machines were bereft of anything remotely healthy. Why do medical staffers chow down on chips, cookies and assorted other crap, while advising our patients to do the opposite?

A beep alerted me to a text. I hoped it wasn't another medical emergency, at least not until I'd consumed something approaching nutrition.

The text bore Tory's name. She was in the lobby. "See U now?"

I sent a thumbs-up and descended from the third floor. Why the visit? Had something happened to Piper?

On a weekend, the lobby drew only a scattering of visitors to the adjacent pharmacy and lab. My tall sister-in-law, in slacks and suit jacket, was pacing near the information desk.

"Hey, doc." She glanced around, but the clerk was busy on the phone and there was no one else nearby. No eavesdroppers, if that was her concern. "Dad said you'd be here."

"News?" I didn't bother with a preamble.

"I was down at the P.D., filling them in about yesterday."

About Piper's visit and the note on her windshield, I presumed. "Filling in who? Trent?"

"Leo," she said. "The whole threat thing was news to him. Piper hasn't stopped in yet."

"That's odd."

"Watch your step, Eric. I have no idea what she's up to, but she could be trying to frame you." Tory's concerned manner contrasted with her usual grouchy attitude toward me.

"Or she may be in trouble." While I bore no fondness for my accuser, I feared she was ignoring a very real danger to herself. She'd been listening to and trusting someone, and that person, judging by the hysterical tone of the note, was growing desperate. "But what brings you here?"

"I ran into Soraya on the way out." Tory paused. About to drop a bombshell?

"Don't keep me in suspense. What did she tell you?"

"Nothing directly." She ducked her head. "I overheard her trying to pry a reaction out of Trent."

"To what?"

"She's uncovered a birth record," Tory said. "And some other stuff."

My breath caught. This wasn't about Piper, but about me. And, more importantly... "Regarding Nicole's baby?"

"Soraya calculates she gave birth seven months after returning to Juneau, which I gather correlates to nine months after your affair."

Mentally, I reviewed the math. "It's off by a few weeks, but the nine-month figure for due dates isn't exact. There really was a girl?"

"Yes. Whoever threatened Piper was on target about that. If she didn't write that note herself."

I dismissed the notion. Unless she was a brilliant actress, Piper's distress had appeared genuine. "Does the birth certificate list the father?"

"It seems not." Tory paused as the lobby doors opened to admit a young couple. "Can we talk somewhere more private?"

"Sure. Why don't we eat lunch? I've been in surgery all morning." While I can go long periods without sleep if necessary, food is another matter. "The cafeteria shouldn't be crowded on the weekend."

"I'll grab a coffee." We set out in that direction. "Trent acted as if he already knew about the birth certificate. Then Soraya got a call from someone and raced out of there."

"Any idea who?"

"Could be a source. Or her boss." Her mouth twisted wryly. "Trent didn't look pleased at her charging off with no explanation."

Inside the cafeteria, the tables were sparsely occupied. While there's no hot food service on the weekend, a case featured a selection of sandwiches and salads. I chose one of each.

The cashier, I saw with a nasty start, was none other than the glowering Yvonne. I handed her cash to cover my food and Tory's drink.

"You should tell the police what you did with that poor little girl," Yvonne muttered as she fiddled with the register.

"Excuse me?"

"Your daughter's missing. You obviously stashed her somewhere. Or her body."

I was too flabbergasted to react. Tory had no such problem. "Who the hell are you?" she demanded.

"She's a mean-spirited snoop who lives to spread gossip," I answered.

Yvonne thrust the change at me. "You should confess what you've done."

I dropped the money into a plastic container soliciting donations for medical research. Not only from generosity; I'd have preferred not to touch it at all.

Tory's face flushed with anger. "You want to kiss your job goodbye?" she snarled. "Quit harassing my brother-in-law."

Yvonne bit her lips.

Tory springing to my defense was a novel experience. "Thanks," I told her when we were clear of the odious cashier.

"She was way out of line."

"I don't think she's familiar with the notion of boundaries." That reminded me a little of Starla, except that she'd never displayed a mean streak.

At a corner table, Tory told me what else she'd overheard from Soraya's conversation with Trent. The child's name was Wendy Blanchard and, according to the reporter, someone at the family's former restaurant in Juneau recalled meeting her as a toddler. The child had last been seen about three years ago, which correlated to the time of Nicole's death.

A lump formed in my stomach. There might be another body under that parking lot, a tiny cluster of bones. But if so, why would the killer be insisting that Piper—or I—disclose the child's whereabouts?

"My client must have been aware she had a niece," Tory fumed. "Surely they met during the three years the little girl lived in Juneau. Damn it!"

Anger welled up in me, too. "Piper dangled the idea of Nicole's pregnancy like bait. She used both of us."

"She's also been withholding information relevant to a homicide," my sister-in-law said. "Since she didn't go to the police with that note from her windshield, I expect they'll be paying her a call."

Despite my fury, I had to credit Piper on one score. "She may believe she's protecting this little girl. Wendy."

Wendy as in *Peter Pan*. Wendy who would be about twelve now, the same age as Fiona from the Labor Day party, the girl with big eyes and a quick mind.

Who had Nicole left her with? Was she safe? When Nicole failed to return, why hadn't the caretaker reported her disappearance? Or had Wendy vanished along with her mother?

My phone rang. Spotting the name on the display, I

answered fast. "Jeremiah?"

"She is gone." He spoke breathlessly.

"What do you mean, gone?"

"Piper has left and taken her things. And that is not all."

"What else?" I didn't pause to explain to Tory. Not yet.

"Eric, I fear I must hire a lawyer," Jeremiah said. "And I advise you to do the same."

CHAPTER ELEVEN

Before driving away, Jeremiah informed me, Piper had recorded a video and sent copies to the media and the police. She claimed to be fleeing for her life from the person who'd killed her sister: Dr. Eric Darcy.

Yes, she'd stated my name flat-out. According to her landlord, she'd provided no evidence to implicate me, aside from the windshield note, which could have been written by anyone. With Jeremiah's permission, investigators were searching his house right now, he told me.

For what? I wondered. Coded messages, computer drives, skeletons in closets, or some scrap of nonsense that might point in my direction?

If they wanted to search my house, they'd have to get a warrant, I resolved. Since a warrant had to specify what they were looking for, I hoped a judge would refuse to issue one. No fishing expeditions on my property, thank you.

From across the cafeteria, I became aware of Yvonne's narrow-eyed stare. However, a flock of chattering customers, pregnant women who had probably been attending a childbirth class, claimed her attention to ring up their purchases.

"The police seem especially interested that I knew Nicole in Boston and was in Safe Harbor when she died," Jeremiah continued over the phone. "They wish me to come in for questioning. I have done nothing wrong."

"You're right. You should get a lawyer." There was no telling what he might say under questioning, in all innocence, or how a jerk like Trent Horner would interpret the fact of Jeremiah's schizophrenia. Ignorance runs rampant about mental illness and the dangers it poses.

Jeremiah has never posed a threat to anyone, in my opinion. He's under the care of a psychiatrist and takes his medication as prescribed. While that doesn't eliminate all symptoms, it does put a damper on them.

When engaged in the practice of medicine, from all accounts he stays focused, and while his cool manner may put off some patients, others appreciate his logical approach. I can testify from having performed operations alongside him that he's a highly skilled surgeon.

"Should I hire the hospital attorney?" he inquired

"No, he isn't a criminal lawyer." I provided the name of one I'd met in Safe Harbor and asked Tory for an additional recommendation, which I shared with him.

"I will hire whoever is immediately available," Jeremiah said.

"Thanks for updating me," I said.

"It is reassuring to have a friend like you to provide advice," he replied.

"We're a mutual aid society."

"That is an accurate metaphor."

As we said goodbye, it occurred to me how much I depended on being surrounded by family and friends who listened, provided insights and sometimes set me straight. Jeremiah had only me as a sounding board. I felt a twinge of guilt at my previous hostility toward him.

"What the hell was that about?" Tory demanded.

When I explained, she scowled and brought up *The Safe Harbor Journal* site on her phone. I did the same.

A video sprang to life, with a caption noting that it had arrived late the previous night. Pale and disheveled, Piper displayed her nervous habits: tugging her hair, straightening her blouse. However, her speech was clear, with no slurring to indicate drugs or alcohol.

"I'm fleeing because I can't wait around for these incompetent Safe Harbor cops to figure out who strangled my sister." She was breathing heavily. "Dr. Darcy is their buddy. They protect their own."

Their buddy? Trent ought to get a laugh out of that one.

"Meanwhile, I'm receiving threats on my life." She held up the now-creased paper that had adorned her windshield.

"Threats, plural?" Tory sniped. "I only count one."

"I'm appealing to the public. Don't let Dr. Eric Darcy get away with murder!"

That was it, the sum total of Piper's manifesto. We watched long enough to catch Soraya's disclaimer.

"The statements made by Dr. Piper Blanchard are purely her own opinions and do not reflect the views of this station," the reporter intoned. "The police have not named a suspect in the murder of Nicole Blanchard, whose remains were uncovered on Tuesday thanks to..." Off she went, recapping the whole process with abundant credit to her employer.

I muted my phone. "How seriously will the detectives take Piper's accusation?"

"They're professionals. They'll follow the evidence," Tory said. "Personally, I don't see why anyone would believe her claims. They're paranoid and unsubstantiated, including the notion that the police are colluding with you."

"I wish I had as much respect for the public." For the moment, the scattering of other diners paid us no attention. That wasn't likely to last.

I kept wishing this mystery would get solved. Instead, it had just blown up even bigger.

Tory rested her chin on the heel of her hand. "I wish I'd never accepted the case. My client was lying from the start."

I didn't bother to point out that that had been obvious to me. Nobody likes to hear I-told-you-so. "To frame me."

"Piper doesn't view it that way, since she's convinced of your guilt," my sister-in-law said. "I was foolish enough to assume that she genuinely wanted the truth."

"You never suspected me?"

"Of being disloyal to Lydia? Yeah, for about five minutes," she said. "Of being a murderer? Never."

"Now what?" I asked. "I mean, how will the police proceed, in your opinion?"

"Depends on what they find at Dr. Schwartz's house, and when they interview him," Tory said. "They've already talked to you, but I'm sure they'll have more questions."

"About the threat on her windshield?"

"And whatever else you might have withheld," Tory murmured.

"I'm not the one withholding stuff," I protested. "Now Piper's in the wind, guarding her secrets." Including clues she might be ignoring because of her blind bias against me. "Do you suppose she knows where Wendy is?"

There'd been no mention of the little girl in her aunt's video. Yet, to me, her safety was paramount.

"Either she does, or whoever appears to be threatening her assumes she does." Tory drummed her fingers on the table. "I'm tending toward your theory that an obsession with the child is the motive behind all this."

My thoughts turned to the latest development. "It can't be easy for Piper to disappear. Everything leaves a trail." No doubt the police were searching her phone and credit card records as well as social media. Running away might not be a crime, but surely they were concerned about her as a missing witness, or potential victim, or... whatever she was. "How far in advance do you suppose she planned this? From the beginning?"

"I don't think so, but at this point, I believe Piper's capable of anything," Tory said. "On the other hand, she could be operating from blind panic."

"Or following instructions."

"That's a possibility."

Clearly she trusted someone—the wrong someone. "The worst part is, she could lead the killer straight to my... to Nicole's daughter."

Tory stared past me toward the entrance. "Well, well, look who just showed up."

I swung around, startled. No, it wasn't Piper. It was Keith.

A few feminine gazes shifted toward him as he advanced across the cafeteria. In jeans and a shirt that emphasized his wide shoulders, my old friend radiated the same blond appeal he'd exerted in high school.

"Eric, you didn't answer my text." He claimed a chair that allowed him a partial view of the entrance. Keith never sits with his back to the door. "A nurse suggested I check the cafeteria."

"I didn't hear the beep." He'd gone to a lot of trouble to locate me by coming here in person, I observed. "What's up? I mean, aside from Dr. Blanchard running off."

"You're current about her video?"

Tory and I both nodded.

Keith kept his voice low. "As you're aware. I can't be involved with this case. But, as a friend, I advise you to go to the station on your own initiative and tell the detectives everything. Right now."

"I did that already, after they dug up Nicole's body," I said. "Aside from unsubstantiated allegations, what's changed?"

"There's a realistic concern about Dr. Blanchard's safety, even though she appears to have left of her own volition," he said. "Have you been at the hospital all morning?"

"Since about eight o'clock," I said.

"Any witnesses before that?"

"Me, at breakfast," Tory said. "He was rooting around in the fridge like a warthog."

I ignored the insult. "Trent saw me out for a jog around seven. He was dropping off his girlfriend at her house."

A few lines eased from Keith's forehead. "That's good."

"They really think I would harm her?"

"Clearly, Dr. Blanchard does."

"She's irrational," Tory put in.

"If she turns up dead, you'd be a logical suspect," Keith told me. "Do you have any sense of who's threatening her?"

"I wish I did."

"Any more patients scheduled?" my friend asked. "If you're free now..."

I sighed. "Guess I should take your advice and head for the station. Again."

"Hire a lawyer," Tory reminded me.

It was the same advice I'd handed out to Jeremiah. Anything I told the detectives could be used against me, especially if Piper got killed. While I had an alibi for this morning, it didn't extend back to the middle of the night, when she'd disappeared.

As with Nicole's death, I could verify where I'd been the evening before and the morning after. but not during the darkest hours. Maybe I should install a time-stamped camera in my bedroom.

Yes, hiring a lawyer would be wise, even though I was innocent. It might also slow down the investigation long enough for the killer to get his hooks into that little girl.

"They're wasting time," I said. "If a lawyer cuts off my statements, they'll keep assuming I'm hiding something."

"Or you'll shoot your mouth off, and they'll seize on a slip of the tongue to hang you out to dry," Tory said fiercely.

"Stay out of this," Keith snapped at her. "Isn't Dr. Blanchard your client?"

"Not any more," she said. "She fired me yesterday."

"Then you have no further business here."

Her jaw tightened. "Aside from the fact that Eric is my brother-in-law."

"That never bothered you before," he pressed. "Something else going on here?"

If Keith wanted her back, he had an odd way of showing it. Tory hates when anyone tries to control her. He should have learned that by now.

"Eric's my new client," she announced.

Keith stared at her. My mouth opened, but I closed it without speaking.

"Has he paid you a retainer?" Keith's attitude reminded me of a terrier his family used to own. Once, the pooch had chomped down on my pants leg, barely missing the flesh, and hung on no matter how hard I shook it, even when I accidentally thumped its butt against a railing.

When he stopped laughing, Keith had lured it away with a treat. After his father learned about the incident, he'd signed them both up for a dog training course. There'd been no further attacks on my leg, although Keith had growled at me a few times, just to yank my chain.

"He's paying me with free rent," Tory flashed at him. "It's a done deal." As if to circumvent any demand for documentary proof, she added, "Handshake."

I didn't contradict her, since she must have realized I'd hold her to it. Thanks to Keith, I had myself a P.I. And he'd done this for no reason other than to satisfy his own mind, since my status as Tory's client had no legal bearing on anything.

"So you're basically working for free?" Keith scoffed.

"Plus expenses," she said.

That seemed fair enough. To Keith, I added, "You'd rather we got to the bottom of this, wouldn't you? Tory's good at her job. Better than Trent, that's for sure."

A shrug indicated he was yielding, however reluctantly. "Don't rely on her, though, Eric. Get ahead of the curve."

I wasn't at all confident that submitting to another interview would put me ahead of anything. Still, it seemed inevitable, and perhaps some useful snippet would emerge. "Okay. I'll do it."

That was how I landed, that afternoon, in a small interview room at the Safe Harbor police department, seated at a plain table bolted to the floor. Recording devices including two video cameras were trained on me, along with the attention of the men sitting opposite: Detective Trent Horner and Sergeant Leo Franco.

I'd come there of my own free will. I quickly began to wish I hadn't.

CHAPTER TWELVE

"Let's talk about your friend, Dr. Jeremiah Schwartz." Due to Trent's pale eyes and lashes, he seemed to regard me without blinking. I felt as if I'd landed on the inside of a fish bowl, with the fish on the outside, studying me. Seated beside him, Sergeant Leo Franco observed us both coolly.

"What about him?" I responded.

"Let's run through how he came to rent a room to Dr. Piper Blanchard," Trent said.

I repeated as many details as I could recall. The nurse/owner's referral. My evening visit to meet the new arrival. Her decision to rent despite learning that a woman had died in the house.

Trent's nostrils flared, which to me signaled skepticism. Leo folded his arms as he listened. I wished I knew Nora's husband well enough to read his reaction.

"And both of you once dated Nicole Blanchard?" Trent queried.

"No." Was he genuinely confused or just fishing?

His eyebrows rose. "You deny having been Nicole Blanchard's boyfriend?"

"You asked about Jeremiah. He was dating Lydia then,

briefly. Lydia Silver, later my wife. I never got the impression he knew Nicole except as a classmate." Was the detective attempting to pin her murder on Jeremiah? Considering that I'd traced that same series of connections, I understood. I didn't like it, though.

"You and he are very close, aren't you?" Trent pressed.

Why was he asking that? "We're friends now. In med school, I disliked him intensely."

The sergeant sparked to life. "Why was that?"

Might as well be frank. "I thought he was creepy and I resented him moving in on Lydia while she and I were taking a break."

"Even though you had a new girlfriend?" Trent challenged.

"I never claimed my reaction was rational."

Tag-teaming, they posed a few more questions as to whether Jeremiah might later have dated Nicole. Since she'd left Boston soon after she and I broke up, I said I considered it unlikely.

"You and Dr. Schwartz later became close, though, didn't you?" Trent continued.

I'd stated that already. "Yes, we're friendlier now."

"Since when?"

"The last year or two."

"Not previously?" Trent was flinging short queries at me, staccato-fashion.

"Definitely not." I didn't grasp why the chronology mattered.

"But prior to that, you both became residents in the same program at UC Irvine, correct?" Leo asked.

"Yes."

"And you entertained him in your home."

That startled me. "My father and I hosted a few gatherings for my fellow residents. Jeremiah attended, along with a bunch of our colleagues. Other than that, no."

"After Nicole Blanchard phoned nine years ago, did you contact him?" Trent demanded.

Leo leaned forward. This must signify something.

"On my wedding night? Why on earth would I?" I amended that to, "No, I did not."

"Did Dr. Schwartz attend your wedding?" the sergeant asked.

Since I hadn't scanned the faces of everyone present, I kept my answer to what I could verify. "He was not on the guest list."

"Why not?" Trent, again.

"Because I thought he was stalking Lydia," I said. "He appeared to be besotted with her."

"With your wife?" A frown crossed Trent's face.

"That's right."

"And was he?"

"No."

"How can you be sure?" he asked.

"According to some research I conducted, Dr. Schwartz's conduct didn't rise, or sink, to the level of stalking." The research had consisted of a conversation with Keith Sparks, but that was none of their business. "Jeremiah later explained that he was watching me and copying some of my choices, such as what kind of car I drive, because he considered me a role model."

Leo spoke up. "Did you and Dr. Schwartz consider Nicole Blanchard a threat to Lydia?"

"Are you kidding?" Obviously, he wasn't. "I'm not sure Lydia and Nicole were even acquainted."

"That doesn't answer the question," the sergeant said.

This was growing weirder and weirder. "Nicole didn't pose a threat to anyone, in my opinion."

"But you and Dr. Schwartz did regard her as a plaything?" Trent put in.

With a jolt, I got a clue what they were hinting at. "You think Jeremiah and I conspired to harm Nicole? That we formulated some bizarre, sadistic plot?"

Neither of them replied. They didn't have to.

"You guys are warped," I told them. "I'm sure this kind of garbage happens. But not to me it doesn't."

I imagined I heard Keith saying, *We have to explore all avenues.* Just doing their job. The problem was that it was taking them far off course.

At a nod from Leo, Trent moved on. Had Nicole sought to blackmail me, to foil my wedding plans with news that I had a child?

"She couldn't have blackmailed me because, if I had a child, I'd want to know him or her, not keep it secret." I heard the edge of anger in my voice. "And where is this kid now while you're wasting time with me?"

Again, no answer.

"Perhaps the events of the past few days have jogged your memory about that night before your wedding," Leo suggested. "Brought up information that hadn't occurred to you before?"

"Unfortunately, no," I said.

"You'd been drinking at a dinner party, right?" Trent put in.

"One glass of champagne. No more." I limit my alcohol intake in case I get called to a medical emergency.

"She must have indicated why she was contacting you," he insisted.

"Not as far as I'm aware." Too irked to be cautious, I shot back, "Would you remember every detail of a brief conversation you had nine years ago?"

"I'd remember anything important and, besides, I'm not the one being questioned here," Trent growled.

"Did you ever travel to Juneau or anywhere else to see Nicole Blanchard?" Leo asked.

"No." I stopped short of telling him to check my credit card records. That might be taken as permission to dig into my personal stuff. Or maybe he'd intended to surprise me, to set me jabbering so I'd reveal a clue.

If I had one, I'd have shared it. But the two of them needed to draw that conclusion on their own.

"Surely there was more to this phone contact," Trent continued doggedly. "Ms. Blanchard came all the way from Alaska. Surely she wouldn't have let you put her off that easily."

"Maybe she had other people to see in this area," I said.

"Such as Dr. Schwartz?"

"You'd have to ask him." I presumed they already had. However, that did remind me of another issue. "Speaking of Jeremiah, he mentioned that Piper occasionally went out to meet friends. Have you identified these friends? Were they also acquaintances of her sister's?"

Leo jotted a note. "Might they be medical colleagues?"

"You'd have to ask the people in her office. Look, someone planted a threat on her windshield, unless she did it herself." Which I doubted. The way she'd stormed into my house waving the paper, she'd either been a brilliant con artist or genuinely angry. "Someone's manipulating her."

"To what end?" Leo asked.

"My guess is that they're fixated on Nicole's child." *Who might also be my child.* "Maybe this person considers himself the real father, or maybe he's a pedophile, or he's obsessed with the girl—Wendy—for reasons of his or her own. Piper said she ran into a cousin who directed her to me. She never specified who that was."

"You think whoever left the note was attempting to trick Dr. Blanchard into revealing the location of her niece?" Leo assumed the lead in the questioning, which was fine with me. I had more respect for his judgment than for Trent's.

"Or to force it out of me, in the belief that I know more than I do," I said. "What if he's tracking Piper right now?"

"Then why did she name you in her video?" Trent demanded.

"Because whoever's manipulating her is very good at it. He's putting the squeeze on both of us. I don't know anything, but maybe Piper does, and she cracked."

If that was true, I hoped her departure had been sudden enough to foil her... what? Stalker? Would-be killer? And that he hadn't accessed the GPS on her car. Because if he had, danger might pursue her far from Safe Harbor.

To a remote area where no one else would spot them. And where law enforcement wasn't easily summoned.

The two men sat for a moment. Absorbing what I'd said, or concluding that I must be the skilled manipulator?

Leo leaned back. "That wraps it up for now."

Since he hadn't turned off the recording devices, I waited.

"One last question."

I braced. When a patient is about to leave and says, often hesitantly, that she has just one more concern, it's often the most important part of the entire exam. "Yes?"

"If we locate Nicole Blanchard's child, would you take a DNA test?"

"Absolutely." As if I weren't dying to confirm or disprove my paternity.

I steamed out of the police station, half wishing I hadn't brought my car. My anger and frustration could have powered me home on foot and burned the edge off my temper.

Had I erred in not bringing a lawyer? At least I should have made my own recording, I reflected, too late. Mentally reviewing what had been said, I didn't believe I'd incriminated myself or Jeremiah, but you can never tell how a prosecutor might twist your words.

I'd always admired those who bring evil-doers to justice. But my sympathy with the falsely accused had risen a few notches today.

No one's accused you of anything, Keith had said. Except now, Piper *had* accused me, publicly. And the cops were floating speculation about a disgusting murder scheme involving me and Jeremiah.

I forced my concentration onto the road. On a warm Saturday afternoon, beach traffic tends to thicken with out-of-towners whose driving habits are unpredictable, and locals whose driving is even more unpredictable. Despite my turbulent emotions and a few abrupt stops, I reached my street without bashing into anyone.

As usual, I tallied the occupants in my house by the presence or absence of cars. No catering truck and no green sedan meant my father-in-law and Tory were both out. However, a battered van at the curb, bearing traces of psychedelic paint from a former owner, indicated my brother-in-law was on the premises. Although he's a successful urologist, Barry is still paying off med school loans and sensible enough not to care about impressing anyone with high-priced wheels.

Inside, the house smelled great. My nose identified maple and bacon.

At the kitchen counter, Barry was using a pastry bag with a special tip to fill egg halves with a yolk mixture. On the counter, two trays of small, sweet-smelling somethings testified to his hard work.

The guy was not only short and sturdy like his father, but also possessed culinary gifts. Had he not become a doctor, he would have been a terrific chef.

"Helping Morris?" I drifted toward the aromas.

"No. My roommate and I are entertaining tonight and he's taken over what passes for a kitchen in our apartment." Barry shared quarters with a fellow urologist. "I promised to fix the hors d'oeuvres. Is it okay, my borrowing your equipment?"

"Sure. It's mostly your father's, anyway." I slid onto a stool and eyed the treats, rather like a dog that sits and points until it's fed. Although my brain sought to conjure up a more dignified approach to presuming on his generosity, it wasn't functioning very well right now.

"Those are maple-caramelized figs topped with bacon." Barry indicated the trays. "Have a couple."

"If you insist."

"Yeah, right." He grinned.

They were beyond delicious. I said so.

"If you don't mind my asking, were you in surgery all day?" he asked as he squirted flower-shaped yellow filling into an egg white. "It's nearly four o'clock."

Unsure how much to lay on him, I said, "No. I had other business to take care of."

"I heard about Dr. Blanchard and her ridiculous claims," my brother-in-law prompted.

"So did the cops." Seizing the chance to vent, I summarized my experience at the P.D. "I respect that they have a job to do, but I'm far from impressed with their attitudes. Especially Trent Horner. He's that pale guy you might have seen on the news."

"Oh, I know who he is. Trent was a year ahead of me in high school." Setting aside the container of finished eggs, Barry stripped off his clear plastic gloves. "I figured he'd go into finance or one of the less reputable specialties of law. I never pictured him as a straight-arrow cop."

"Why not?" I cheerfully accepted the egg half he offered me.

The yolk mixture had been augmented with onion and a touch of apple. Cider vinegar, perhaps.

"He's always been opportunistic. Not somebody I'd trust with my life." He paused and, in that hesitation, I gathered he was weighing whether to share more.

On the surface, my brother-in-law presents as an easygoing fellow, but there are depths. "I'd appreciate whatever insights you can offer."

"I was wondering if I should talk to you or to my sister about this," Barry said. "It might be nothing."

"About what? When it comes to this investigation, nothing's nothing." I kept sensing undercurrents. Perhaps he'd puzzled out one of them.

Barry donned a second set of gloves. "You know that new young woman at the cafeteria, Keely's cousin?"

"Starla," I said. "She's dating Trent."

"I heard that." His forehead furrowed. "She got real friendly at lunch yesterday."

"With you or with everybody?"

"With me."

"Was she flirting?" I wouldn't put it past the woman, despite her relationship with Trent. "Starla has no filter."

"It was more calculated than that." Barry began fitting the fig-bacon treats into a plastic container. "I was alone on the patio, finishing my meal, when she plopped down next to me. She handed me a chocolate-chip muffin I'd been eyeing earlier and said it was good for me. Seriously, a chocolate-chip muffin?"

"And?" Clearly there was more.

"She started pumping me for information about you." Barry measured a precise layer of parchment paper to cover the figs. "Had you discussed having a daughter? Did you travel out of town a lot? That kind of thing."

"Did you ask her why?"

"She claimed it was simple curiosity," he said. "Damn it, Eric, do you think that weasel Trent is using her to snoop? I wouldn't put it past him."

About to dismiss the idea as far-fetched, I recalled my missing and possibly purloined sports watch, and told him about it. "I hate to think a police detective would stoop that low."

"On the other hand, we are talking about Trent Horner," Barry said. "In computer class, he talked my friend Parker into teaming with him on a project. Parker did all the work, even fixing Trent's lousy coding. But Trent took half the credit."

"Did Parker tell the teacher?"

A shake of the head. "Even though he complained about it to me, he didn't bother. Parker has nothing to prove, since he's a genius."

I wondered how a bottom feeder like Trent had survived modern police-screening methods in a metropolitan area, where applicants were presumably held to high standards. By never having been caught or reported for unethical behavior, I supposed.

We were still dissecting Trent's lack of character when Tory arrived home. She proved more than happy to sample her brother's wares.

"How'd you survive the interview?" she asked me.

"That remains to be seen." I recalled that I'd left her in the cafeteria with her ex-boyfriend. "Did Keith hang around?"

"Like an albatross."

"What's the state of the relationship?" Barry inquired in his low-key manner.

"He's a mess." From the fridge, Tory retrieved a beer. "He has no idea what he wants. For me to stay away from anything involving you, Eric, but also to keep you from being railroaded."

"By Trent?"

"Who else?"

"Keith's sharp," Barry observed. "I doubt he has a high opinion of that slime bucket, either."

"Wow, that's the nastiest thing I've ever heard you say about anybody." Tory settled beside me at the counter. "What brought that up?"

Barry explained about his high school experience with Trent and his run-in with Starla. Then, at his sister's request, I recounted my interview and the detectives' perverted speculation about Jeremiah and me.

Tory's chin jutted in a familiar bulldog effect. "Did you share your theory about a father-figure pursuing Nicole's daughter?"

"Yes. As far as I could tell, they blew it off," I said. "Also, during the interview, it occurred to me that the killer might be tracking Piper's car. If that's true, she's in a lot of danger."

"Let's hope they're on top of that," Tory said.

"They must have a lot of possibilities to pursue." Her brother snapped a lid on the last of his plastic containers, conserving the diminished supply of hors d'oeuvres.

"I'll grant you, their resources are limited." Tory rested her elbows on the counter. "A nine-year-old murder doesn't warrant assigning a big task force or calling in reinforcements from another police agency."

"What about the kid?" Wendy was my main concern, assuming she was alive and hadn't been put up for adoption as a baby.

"The fact that we haven't located her doesn't mean she's been harmed," Tory pointed out. "Piper's presumably the next of kin, yet as far as I can tell, she never filed a missing person report about her niece."

"She could be on her way to see Wendy now." I had a bad feeling about that. "With a killer on her trail."

Barry studied us both. "I can see why you guys get obsessed with these cases."

"We aren't obsessed," Tory and I said almost in unison.

"Of course not." My brother-in-law slid the food into a shopping bag. "Enjoy your evening."

"Have fun at your party," I said.

With a wave, he was gone.

Morris blew in soon afterwards with extra meals from his deliveries, and the three of us ate in the great room as we watched movies on the large screen. One comedy featured animals—Morris's choice—followed by an action film selected by his daughter. I was too distracted by the day's events to pay much attention.

On Sunday, I slept late. When I went downstairs, I discovered a note from Tory atop the breakfast table.

"Flying to Alaska," she wrote. "Glad you're paying expenses."

I hoped her trip proved worthwhile. And that she wasn't putting herself in the path of a killer.

CHAPTER THIRTEEN

"I'm beginning to wonder if I'm cursed," Dr. Chuck Kane told Jeremiah and me over sandwiches in the doctors' lounge on Tuesday. "You left my practice on good terms, Jer, but Alison died and now Piper's, well...I'm hoping for the best, but the bottom line is, she's gone."

Nervously, our colleague stroked his chin, which today seemed to reach an even sharper point than usual. He'd served in the Army, which had paid for his medical school, before buying into an obstetrical practice a few years ago. Other than that, I knew little about him except that he was in his early forties and divorced with a young daughter. He had got along well with Jeremiah, who'd left a couple of years ago to open his own office down the hall from mine.

We were avoiding the cafeteria due to the inevitable staring and whispering following this morning's news. Piper's car had been discovered in the parking lot of a Las Vegas motel. Apparently she'd completed the five-hour drive but never checked in.

Had she met someone by arrangement? Had she been abducted? Police were keeping a lid on the details. I had no clue how seriously they were taking her absence. Until now, her departure had seemed to be voluntary. However, this latest development struck me as troubling.

That morning, Jeremiah and I had each covered a couple of her scheduled surgeries, in addition to our own. Patients' needs don't disappear simply because a physician goes missing. They'd become Chuck's responsibility, since he owned the practice, and we'd rallied around him, as he would have done for us.

I was grateful for the refuge provided by the lounge. The story had grown to the point that I could hardly listen to my car radio without hearing call-ins spewing conspiracy theories. Today, there'd been a crazy lady declaring, "I had Dr. Darcy's baby!" I hoped that wasn't about to turn up as a headline in supermarket tabloids.

A pediatrician popped in to fill her mug from the coffee pot. After casting us a sympathetic smile, she departed.

"Would you restore Dr. Blanchard's position if she requests it?" Jeremiah inquired.

Chuck shrugged, his narrow face set in its customary worried expression. In fairness, I'd mostly viewed him during crises, which, as he'd noted, hit him all too often.

"I have to start recruiting for a new doctor," he said. "It's a slow process, but once someone signs a contract, I'll no longer require her services."

Rising, we tossed our rubbish in the trash can. As we passed a wall mirror, I was caught by the image of three doctors in our midthirties, superficially similar yet strongly dissimilar in the details. Our brown hair ranged in texture from tightly curly—Jeremiah's—to *goyishe* thick and straight, as my late wife used to describe mine, to thinning. Chuck's white coat hung loose on his slender frame; I was taller and sturdier at five-eleven, while Jeremiah stooped as if self-conscious about towering over us.

My patients often cite body image concerns, especially when changes occur due to pregnancy, age or illness. Meanwhile, the pervasive media visuals of young, photo-retouched models daunt even the most self-confident. Women have my sympathy, and I do my best to reassure them. The truth is, men rarely worry about such things, or at least, I don't.

Downstairs, we exited via a staff door into a reserved parking lot. Single-file, we passed a flowering hedge that sheltered the cafeteria's patio, hearing the clink of plates and glasses from lunch in full swing.

With luck, we might escape unnoticed, Jeremiah and me to the adjacent building, Chuck to his car and a short drive to his office. Luck, however, was not with us.

Near the corner to the main walkway lingered a cameraman, whose fervent gesture brought the beautiful but annoying Soraya bearing down. "Doctors!" Her gleeful smile shaded into a semblance of concern. "Have you received any word from Dr. Blanchard?"

We shook our heads.

"What do you suppose happened to her?" She blocked our escape.

On camera, we could hardly elbow her out of our path, not that any of us would get into a shoving match off camera, either. Still, it was tempting.

"Excuse us," I said. "We have patients to see."

"Dr. Darcy!" She practically squealed my name. "Surely you're desperate to discover what's become of your daughter."

It was a good thing I'd jammed my hands into my pockets so she couldn't see the fists. "My paternity has not been established."

A rustling from the hedge drew my attention. For once, it was a relief to spot a chunky figure with pink-and-blue hair scrambling toward us. The odor of cigarettes wafted around her, although smoking wasn't allowed in the hospital.

"Ms. Montenegro!" Starla burst out. "You're asking exactly the questions the public wants to know. What has Dr. Darcy done with his little girl?"

Not such a relief, after all.

Soraya's dark eyes blazed. "Yes, I was discussing that with him before you interrupted."

The newcomer faced the camera with a perky smile. "Hi, I'm Starla Randolph, and I'm really close to this case. I clean Dr. Darcy's house and boy, if you ask me, there's plenty I could tell."

Anger overrode my judgment. "Does it have anything to do with a sports watch someone stole from my bedroom? Not that it contained any revealing information, but the thief may have believed it did."

In my peripheral vision, I saw Chuck slipping away. Good. No reason for him to get trapped in the line of fire.

Jeremiah stuck by me.

"I'm not a thief, I'm an investigator!" Starla huffed. "I'm assisting a person close to the case."

I'd have liked to see Trent's face when he heard that.

"Ms. Randolph, the *Journal* values the public's input." Soraya appeared to be barely hanging onto her temper. "However, please allow me to finish interviewing the doctor before I speak with you."

"Afraid of competition?" challenged the newcomer. "Maybe I'm the one who should be on camera."

Soraya's jaw dropped. I didn't recall ever before seeing her speechless. From her rigid body language, I suspected she'd have liked to karate-chop Starla to oblivion, but this was presumably a live feed.

Again, the bushes parted and another yellow-uniformed figure thrust through it. Ah, here came Starla's large-headed, big-mouthed buddy. I tensed for whatever insult Yvonne Worth might hurl at me.

Instead, she confronted her friend. "Your break is over and we're busy. Get your butt inside."

Starla's nostrils flared. "You can't order me around. I have inside info."

An irritated exhalation indicated Soraya was still struggling with how to handle this awkward scene. The cameraman raised an eyebrow but, in the absence of any indication to stop, kept shooting.

Yvonne's lip curled. "Everyone's sick of hearing about how your boyfriend is a cop. As for this inside info, why haven't you shared that with him already?"

"Maybe I will."

"And maybe you're bluffing."

"Hey, I know more than you think," her target declared. "Secrets don't stay secrets forever."

The older woman grabbed her elbow. While they glared at each other, Jeremiah and I strode past the reporter.

Saved by the hellions.

I've never understood the hunger for notoriety that propels some folks to crave even the most unflattering attention. Perhaps it's an inborn trait, useful for those with performing talent or political ambition. For most, I mused as I escaped to my office, it reflects a longing to be acknowledged as valuable and special. Most importantly, real.

Without a spotlight, I cast no shadow.

Well, Starla wasn't my problem, aside from the possibility that she'd stolen my watch. Today, she'd done me an unintended favor by distracting the press.

Later, well past the dinner hour, my rumpled sister-in-law returned from her travels. She joined me in my second-floor library.

Tory's texts had kept me informed that she was visiting both Juneau, where the Blanchard girls had grown up, and Anchorage, where Piper had practiced medicine. Beyond that, I presumed there'd been no bombshell discoveries or she'd have communicated them already.

Before discussing her trip, we exchanged the latest kernels gleaned from various sources about Piper's disappearance. There wasn't much. Aside from the news that her luggage had also disappeared and that there were no obvious signs of a struggle, police in Las Vegas and Safe Harbor were sticking to their still-under-investigation line.

With her picture plastered across screens and social media throughout the region, Piper would almost certainly be identified if she showed up in public, nor would she dare use her phone or credit cards. Since she'd been missing for more than forty-eight hours, Tory agreed with me that this had either been a well-planned escape or something much darker.

Considering that she'd been hiding details about Nicole, our thoughts ran along the something-darker line. But whether she was being manipulated by the killer or by her own disordered mind remained an open question.

"Dig up anything useful in Alaska?" I stretched along the sofa. The library, which doubled as a game room, was a soothing spot. When my wife redecorated the house, she preserved the dark woods and high shelves, many of the classic books and the kitschy mugs and other mementos from my parents' travels.

"I may have identified a trail," Tory said from an easy chair. "Except I'm not sure where it will lead."

"What kind of trail?"

"The faint and winding kind."

"Start with Juneau." Except for a vague awareness that the city had its origins in a late 19th-century gold rush and was a popular cruise ship port of call, I knew almost nothing about Alaska's state capital. Not that I expected a travelogue.

My sister-in-law plucked open a small pack of potato chips. While I disliked having people drop crumbs in the upholstery, no doubt Starla would vacuum them out as she searched the cushions for incriminating clues.

"The family restaurant, Blanchard's, still operates under that name, although it's changed owners several times." Crunch, crunch.

She had, naturally, omitted to bring a napkin for her oily hands. I handed her a tissue.

"Most of the staff is short-term, May to September." Tory executed a desultory wipe worthy of a six-year-old. "Something like a million tourists swarm the city during those months. The rest of the year, the population hovers around thirty thousand."

I wished she'd cut to the chase, but she looked too drained to whittle down her story without prodding. "Any old-timers who remembered the Blanchards?"

"One grizzly guy named, of course, Gus," she said.

"Why `of course'?"

"Aren't all grizzly old guys named Gus?"

I chose not to argue. "Was he the chatty type?"

"To put it mildly."

More crunching followed. I wondered if she'd skipped dinner. "Did he share anything worthwhile?"

She smiled wearily. "Perhaps. The late Mrs. Blanchard had a close friend who used to manage the restaurant."

This person must know about Nicole's years in that city, including her pregnancy. "Male or female?"

"Female."

"Still living?"

"Unclear." She stretched her shoulders. "Gus wasn't sure of

her name but it might have been Bonnie or Bernice."

"What happened to her?" I prodded.

"You're getting ahead of me."

"Sorry."

From the pack, she fished a wad of broken chips, sprinkling bits around her as she stuffed them into her mouth. After a bit of chewing, she said, "According to Gus, Bonnie or Bernice was like an aunt to the Blanchard girls. She was close to Nicole after her mother died. Might have helped care for the baby."

My breath caught at this hint about my maybe-daughter's childhood. Until now, she'd been little more than a name. She'd had a babysitter, a grandmotherly type who might have heard her first words, witnessed her first steps. "What happened to the woman?" I repeated.

"Gus hasn't seen her or the little girl in a while."

"Months? Years?"

"He was fuzzy on specifics."

How frustrating. "Had anyone else at the restaurant heard of her?"

"The names Bonnie and Bernice failed to ring so much as a wind chime."

"She has to be somewhere." Idiotic remark, I recognized, and hurried on. "Maybe Nicole left Wendy with this friend while she flew down here to talk to me. Any chance the woman filed a missing person report when Nicole didn't return?"

"Not according to the local constabulary," Tory said. "Who have very nice manners, by the way."

Ramifications kept occurring to me. "If this woman was close to the family, Piper must have known her."

"Obviously, yes. And I'll be happy to quiz the good doctor when she surfaces."

If she was still alive. *Don't go there.*

That brought me back to the motherly friend. "Did Gus have

any idea where Bonnie or Bernice might have gone? A hometown, perhaps?"

"The difficulty is, he kept confusing her with a cousin of the Blanchards' whose name, he swore, sounded like Bernie, but wasn't." Tory set aside the empty package. "So we have a Bonnie or Bernice and a not-quite-Bernie."

"Also female?"

"Yes."

"Are you sure they aren't the same person?"

"Not sure of anything." She yawned.

Generally, I'm sympathetic to an exhausted, hungry person. However, I'd run out of patience. "And?"

"My next stop was Anchorage."

"Any more guys named Gus?" I hoped she'd discovered a more helpful source.

"No, but Piper's coworkers were concerned enough to talk freely," Tory said. "The police had been in touch, so they'd learned she was missing."

"Any ideas where she might be?"

"Not exactly." Tory checked her notes. "Piper practiced there for around four years. In addition to treating patients in Anchorage, she flew to remote villages and small clinics to provide care, which was how she met the pilot she was dating."

That got my full attention. According to Piper's colleagues, the man had been a charmer who took advantage of his high-flying lifestyle. Then, six or seven months ago, Piper had treated a pregnant woman who turned out to be his wife.

Rather than ditch the jerk, the wife had insisted they move to her home state of Hawaii. And there they'd gone, greatly diminishing the likelihood that Don Juan had played a role in Piper's subsequent troubles. Nevertheless, to nail down his whereabouts, Tory had contacted the wife. Once she recovered from her annoyance, the woman had confirmed that her husband was indeed living with her in the Aloha State.

My brain sketched a timeline. Piper had arrived in Anchorage roughly four years ago, which meant Nicole must have been dead for five years already. Still, perhaps Bonnie/Bernice and Wendy had also moved there. "She didn't introduce her coworkers to her niece, by chance? Or mention her?"

A shake of the head dispensed a few crumbs that had clung to my sister-in-law's face. "Nope, but Piper had a former roommate from Seattle who visited her a while back. One of the nurses provided the friend's name. Dr. Heidi Jensen."

I swung my legs to the floor. "Did you reach her?"

"All they had was an email address." Tory blew out a breath. "I couldn't locate any more information under that name. Maybe she got married. I wish women would stop changing their names. It makes them hard to track."

"You emailed her?"

"No answer so far, although it didn't get kicked back by the Mailer Daemon. Nothing on social media, either."

That didn't surprise me, since doctors tend to be careful about how we interact with the public. "Surely when she reads the message, she'll be worried enough about Piper to get in touch with you."

"If she still uses that address. Or isn't already involved. Maybe Piper's staying with her." Another yawn. "I'm going to bed now. Or food. No, bed. Tomorrow, I'll share this with the cops, for whatever it's worth."

Despite the urge to squeeze more out of her, I acknowledged the futility. If she'd overlooked something in her exhaustion, it wouldn't surface until morning. And maybe tomorrow we'd get a response from the roommate.

I thanked Tory for her work. She'd mined some nuggets up there in Alaska. A grandmotherly friend who might be safeguarding the little girl. A former roommate whom Piper might contact if she were desperate.

None of this explained why Nicole had left her daughter and flown to Safe Harbor to talk to me. Nor why, if you could trust what Piper claimed to have learned from a cousin, Nicole had believed she was in danger. Nor, now that I thought about it, who that mysterious cousin might be.

That night, I dreamed of brown bears named Bonnie, Bernie and Bernice closing in on a little girl, alone and terrified in a forest. I was struggling to get to her, caught by brambles and vines, when the phone jarred me from sleep.

The bedside clock showed 4:14 a.m. An emergency with a patient? Not pausing to check the readout, I answered. "Eric Darcy."

"Dr. Darcy! I didn't know who else to call!" It was an older woman's hoarse, familiar voice. "They found her body. I can't believe it!"

"What? Who is this?" I strained to penetrate my sleep-infused bewilderment. "Keely?"

"Yes, yes, it's me." Labored breathing. "The coroner needed her next-of-kin contact. I'm the closest relative in Safe Harbor, so they called me. She's dead, Dr. Darcy!"

Why on earth would the authorities drag Keely into this? "Piper's dead?"

"No!" Her voice cracked. "Eric, it's Starla! Somebody killed Starla!"

CHAPTER FOURTEEN

While I strained to control my shock, Keely rattled on. "If not for me, she'd have stayed in Utah. She'd be safe now!"

"You can't know that," I said numbly.

"It's that damn DNA test. When you apply, they warn you might be opening a can of worms, but who lets that stop them?" She rolled onward. "I feel awful! I was wishing she'd go home. I thought she was irritating. Do you suppose that's why she got killed?"

"People don't usually kill someone just because they're annoying," I said. "If they did, most of us would no longer be walking around."

In my stunned state, I couldn't think how to proceed. Luckily, my sister-in-law padded in, hair frizzing like a lion's mane above the tank top and gym shorts she'd worn to bed. "What's up?" she mouthed.

"Starla's dead." I put the phone on speaker. "Keely, Tory just walked in."

"I'm sorry about your cousin, Keely." Tory sat beside me on the bed. "How did she die?"

"She was murdered! I can't believe it!" Her voice grew more agitated with every word.

Gently, Tory said, "Tell us what happened."

"I don't know where to start."

"At the beginning. There's no hurry."

"Okay. Okay."

Slowly, Keely related the circumstances. An officer on patrol had observed Starla's car parked near the end of Pelican Lane, half a block from their home. Since that was an isolated location, he'd stopped to check and spotted her body slumped over the steering wheel with her neck at an odd angle.

The grim account felt surreal. The words shattered the peace of my bedroom, which my wife had decorated in soothing shades of tan and beige and lilac. Murder had once again struck close to home.

Keely's remarks veered into regrets. "I didn't hear a thing. If I'd gone out and looked, maybe I could have saved her."

"Or maybe you'd be dead, too," Tory countered. "Was her neck broken? You said it was at an odd angle."

"Maybe." Keely blew her nose. That had only a minimal effect on the nasal quality when she resumed. "The patrolman thought she'd been strangled. Then another officer came by and told him to clap a lid on it." For police, I've heard, information is supposed to flow only in one direction—to them, not from them—except when it's necessary to brief the next of kin.

The indication that there'd been another strangling, even years after Nicole's, disturbed me intensely. It might indicate the killer was still active. Unless the coroner ruled that she'd died from some other cause, such as a seizure. Had Starla used drugs? Did she suffer from epilepsy?

"When was the last time you saw Starla?" Tory asked.

"Around seven last night."

"Did she say what her plans were?" I joined in. "Or where she was going?"

"She was meeting friends." Keely sniffed. "I went to bed around ten and she was still out, but that's not unusual."

I'd run out of queries. "Have the police interviewed you yet?" Tory asked.

"Well, the patrolman did, a little. Like, had I seen or heard anything unusual. I wish I had!"

"Don't discuss this with anyone else until the detectives interview you." Tory didn't appear remorseful for questioning the witness, only cautious. "Write down everything you remember about last night, so you don't get it mixed up with anything you hear or speculate."

"What if they ask about private stuff?" Keely was winding up again. "About Starla, I mean. Personal details she wouldn't have wanted to share with other people."

Such as that Starla was sleeping with one of the detectives? I wondered. Or was there more?

"Don't hide anything," Tory said. "You can never tell what might be important."

"What if they don't believe me?" she burst out. "What if they think I'm involved? I'm the one who invited her to live here!"

"You've done nothing wrong, Keely," I said.

"People tend to think the worst of me." Her abrasive manner hadn't won her many friends over the years.

"You're not responsible for this," Tory said. "All you need to do is be truthful."

"And go easy on yourself. This is a traumatic experience. Call in sick to work," I advised.

"I can't do that. Dr. Brennan counts on me." As a nurse, she assisted Dr. Paige Brennan, one of my fellow OBs.

"Tell her what happened to your cousin," I said. "She'll understand. Under these conditions, you can't be expected to focus one hundred percent on your patients."

Finally, Keely agreed and said goodbye. By this point, the

rest of her household must be awake and curious. Horrified, too, when they learned the cause of the commotion on their street.

Downstairs, Tory and I chewed over the situation along with our breakfast. She still had to brief the detectives regarding what she'd discovered in Alaska, she noted. However, in view of this latest development, that faint trail and the tangle of similarly named friends and cousins might not strike them as a priority.

What did it mean if the two murders were linked? Despite the passage of years and the possibility of a coincidence, I presumed they were, since Starla had been sticking her nose into the missing-child business. She'd claimed on camera that she was assisting a person close to the case.

When I mentioned that to Tory, she grimaced. "Seriously?"

"You didn't see Soraya's latest newscast?"

"I must have missed it while I was in transit." She clicked to the *Journal* site on her phone. "Yep, they're running the video."

"I'm in it, too," I observed. Unnecessarily, since she would soon witness for herself my awkward appearance.

Tory listened to the exchange. "I'd forgotten about your missing sports watch. In case it turns up in her possession, it's a good thing you brought it up already."

"You mean, I might be suspected again?" I shook my head in disgust.

Tory's fingers drummed on the table. "Since Trent was dating her, they'll have to remove him from the case."

"Could he be a suspect?" I wondered.

"Everybody's a suspect."

Spoken like an experienced cop. "Why would he kill her?"

"On that video, Starla went public about their snooping," she said. "Assuming she was colluding with Trent, he might have lost his temper. People have been murdered for less."

That would mean the slayings were only superficially linked. I considered the scenario unsatisfying. "What if there's a deeper connection?"

"Such as?"

A memory surfaced, something Starla had told me. "She met Trent at the Suncrest Saloon."

"So?" Tory studied me dubiously.

While this speculation might be far-fetched, it was just my sister-in-law and me, talking. "Maybe he met Nicole there, too. After she talked to me, she might have gone out for a drink. And she liked to dance."

"Eric, that's quite a stretch," she said. "Was Trent even in Safe Harbor nine years ago?"

"He grew up here." In my eagerness to speak, a bit of croissant stuck in my throat. I coughed, swallowed, and downed a mouthful of coffee before continuing. "He was a year behind you in high school."

"You remember him? Because I don't," Tory muttered.

"No, but Barry does. According to your brother, he wasn't very ethical." In fairness, I added, "But that hardly qualifies him as a serial killer."

"We aren't dealing with a serial killer, not by the classic definition." Tory went to pour herself a second, or third, cup of coffee. From the counter, she explained, "To qualify, there should be three or more murders, with a psychological motive, and maybe sadistic sexual overtones. Even if the same person murdered Nicole and Starla, the stranglings strike me as impulsive, rather than planned. Could be thrill killings, I suppose, but nine years is a long gap. Assuming there aren't other cases that we've missed."

"That doesn't rule him out, though." Suppose a drunken Trent had raped or attempted to rape Nicole, and feared she would report him to the police? And suppose Starla had threatened to claim publicly that she'd stolen my watch at his direction? "You think Leo will take a hard look at him?"

"Leo's a good cop." Tory rejoined me at the table. "With two detectives compromised in such a small department, they ought to hand this over to another agency, but the chief's possessive about his city. I'm guessing he'll ask Lieutenant Hough to help with the investigation."

"Huff?" The name didn't ring a bell.

"Spelled like Tough," she said. "Only, in truth, Ed's kind of a paper shuffler."

"Meaning?"

"Good at digging through reports and spotting mistakes," she said. "Especially dry technical ones."

"That can be useful. Studying charts when there's been an adverse patient outcome is important." As was my habit, I drew parallels between police work and the practice of medicine. Safe Harbor MC regularly assessed mortality and morbidity, especially when there was an unexpected death or major complication. As a result, we were continually improving our treatments and processes.

"Doctors make mistakes?" Tory gibed. "Better not tell the malpractice attorneys."

"Don't get me started on that subject." Enough chatter. "Gotta go."

"Busy day for me, too." Sharing her findings with the police, as she'd indicated. And Tory presumably had other cases, insurance fraudsters and cheating spouses, that paid the bills.

Over the next few hours, I struggled to keep from dwelling on the tragedy. Not an easy task in the gossip mill that surrounded me. During the week she'd worked at the cafeteria, Starla had become a familiar figure to many. Unlike Nicole's murder, this one seemed personal to the staff.

Even my usually self-contained partner, Dr. Isaiah Levin,

commented on it. "This kind of thing didn't used to happen around here. In my day, Safe Harbor lived up to its name." His day had been a few decades past, when he'd launched this practice with my father.

"Orange County's had its share of notorious criminals," I couldn't resist pointing out. "The Freeway Killer, the Night Stalker."

"They didn't operate in Safe Harbor. And they committed crimes in LA, too."

Still, in the last few years, we'd seen a spike in the local murder rate. Although the victims hadn't been chosen at random, I failed to find that reassuring. For instance, doctors have been slain by paranoid patients. Being targeted because your treatment failed can still be fatal.

At the reception desk, Glenda kept her phone on the news feed, despite a few rebukes from my nurse. By late afternoon, as the waiting room emptied, she turned up the volume on a Los Angeles TV station. I couldn't resist pausing to watch.

No doubt against departmental policy, Trent had spoken with a reporter who cornered him on the steps of the police department. Peppered with questions about dating the victim, he said, "We went out a few times, but whoever she was snooping for, it wasn't me. That would be unethical and unfair to Starla."

"Were you in love with her?" the reporter asked.

To my surprise, the man's eyes brimmed. "She was a lot of fun, a bright spirit. That's all I have to say."

Waving off further inquiries, Trent hurried away. Grieving, or faking?

Shortly before six p.m., I was preparing to leave when a blunt-featured man in his mid-forties stepped into the patient-free waiting room. Spotting me through the reception window, he said, "Dr. Darcy?"

"Yes." Might have been a patient's husband, but my mind leaped to the investigation. "And you are?"

"Lt. Ed Hough, Safe Harbor police." He issued the statement with a weary air. He appeared fit enough to take down a resisting perp, but I guessed he hadn't had to tackle anyone in years.

I went to shake hands with the lieutenant. "You're here about Starla Randolph?"

He nodded. "Mind answering a few questions down at the station?"

After a long day, I had no interest in being dragged in for questioning if I had a choice. Since I gathered that I did, I said, "I'll talk to you here. Take it or leave it."

"All right." If Hough was offended, he didn't show it.

In my private office, we both took seats. As he produced a recording device, I asked, "Did you drive over here just to talk to me?" Considering his earlier request that I come to the station, it would have been more sensible to phone first.

"To you and others at the hospital who knew the victim."

Which others? I didn't bother to ask, since he'd never have told me. Cafeteria staff, I presumed, and perhaps those who worked with Keely.

For the recording, the lieutenant stated his name, along with the time, date and place, and had me identify myself. "When did you last see Miss Randolph?"

"Yesterday. It's on that video the *Journal* is running." I presumed he'd watched it, more than once.

"Not later?"

"No."

"How about running through your whereabouts for the rest of the day?"

I explained that I'd been here until six-ish, returned home, then met with my sister-in-law. And no, I hadn't gone out again that evening.

As I spoke, the lieutenant jotted notes, in addition to the recording. A paper-shuffler, Tory had described him. Mild-mannered but not weak, I judged from his steady manner.

"On the video, you spoke of a missing sports watch," Hough said. "What sort of information did it contain?"

"My heart rate and jogging route," I said. "It could also access my calendar and some financial data. I deactivated it immediately."

"Why would anyone steal it, other than for financial gain?"

About to reply that I had no idea, I realized he'd brought up a key point. "To trace my movements. I have a theory these murders might have been committed by someone fixated on Nicole Blanchard's daughter."

"Was she your daughter?" His tone remained bland.

"I have no idea." I resumed my thread. "Whoever's doing this might believe I know where the child is, which I don't. But if I did, tracking my whereabouts over the past few days could have provided a clue. Did you find it, by the way?"

"Find what?"

"The watch."

"I'm not at liberty to say."

My guess was that they hadn't, or he'd ask for the password in case he might still be able to access its data. However, I seized the chance to capitalize on Lieutenant Hough's presumed talents with paperwork.

"How deeply have you explored Starla's background?" I asked. "If the killer wasn't Detective Horner"—his hand jerked at that—"why would someone choose her to spy on me?"

"She did work for you as a housecleaner," Hough noted.

"And who would she trust enough to snoop for them, besides Trent Horner? Could it be Dr. Blanchard?" Nine years ago, I calculated, Starla would have been around twenty-one, living in Utah. No obvious connection to Piper, but who else did this leave?

"Have you seen or spoken to Dr. Blanchard since she left?"

"No, but she could have dumped her car in Vegas and doubled back." I wouldn't put anything past Nicole's sister, whether it was stealing a car or murdering an accomplice who proved inconvenient. "Do you have any sense of where she is?"

"I assure you, we're following every lead."

"Was any of her DNA in Starla's car?" I demanded. "Have you found any references to Nicole's daughter among Starla's possessions?"

"Dr. Darcy, I'm the one posing questions here."

I wasn't about to back off, not in my current mood. "Have you asked Starla's parents if she mentioned who her friends were, here in Safe Harbor? Any clue who she was meeting the night she died?"

Impatiently, the lieutenant ended the recording. "Thank you for your time, doctor. Please call if you remember anything else." Handing me his card and pocketing his recorder, he headed for the door.

In my impatience, I'd overstepped and probably alienated the man. Nevertheless, I held out the slim hope that the lieutenant's penchant for details might reveal a link others had missed.

CHAPTER FIFTEEN

As events played out, we uncovered our own new information almost immediately. I was sliding into my car when a text beeped.

From Tory: "Get home now!"

Specifics would have been nice. However, perhaps my sister-in-law was in a dangerous situation or had a visitor she didn't care to tip off.

Driving as fast as safety allowed, I did my best not to speculate about what lay ahead. Instead, the encounter with Lieutenant Hough dominated my musings. What had he learned, if anything, from other hospital staffers? Not enough to pose any startling questions to me, I gathered, although I was sure a few of them had dropped unflattering comments.

I toyed with scenarios of him querying the dislikable Ms. Worth, who'd likely stabbed at him with needle-sharp rumors. I doubted that her friend's murder had dimmed her love of gossip.

In the garage, I slotted my car next to my sister-in-law's and hurried to her bay-windowed office. The computer screen had been swiveled to face the guest side where, seated in a padded chair, Tory had stretched her long legs and plopped her feet on the desk. A keyboard rested on her knees.

"Five minutes." She indicated for me to occupy the chair beside her.

"Until?" Heart rate pumping, hands prickling from suspense, I stood ready to propel myself into whatever action lay ahead.

"Seven."

"Seven o'clock?" *Okay, Eric, figure it out.* I settled beside her. "Who are we video conferencing with?"

"Dr. Heidi Jensen."

Names paraded through my head. Ah, Piper's roommate. "She contacted you?"

"She read my email and phoned half an hour ago."

"You could have simply told me that. I thought the roof had caved in," I grumbled.

"Don't whine, Eric."

"What did she say?"

At a gallop, Tory summarized: "She lives in Florida. It's 10 p.m. there. New baby. Had to finish nursing. Dermatologist, kept her maiden name. Shocked about Nicole. Hasn't heard from Piper."

That packed in a lot of details. "Must have been some conversation."

"Interrupted by mommy duty. Also, she's curious about you. Agreed to video chat at... now!"

The strain to shift gears and concentrate on the interview ahead reminded me of my emergency-room rotation while in training. On a busy night, you had to rush from one patient to another, assessing urgent needs, the extent of injuries, the significance of a rash or fever, and the advisability of ordering expensive tests that might bankrupt a person or save his life, or both. Mental gymnastics had been relatively easy in my late twenties. A decade later, not as much.

I concentrated on the image that appeared before us, a round face crowned by short, curly brown hair. Piper's old friend looked solemn, but friendly.

"Greetings from Florida." The woman grimaced. "Darn, I sound like one of those tourist postcards. Hi again, Tory. And you must be Eric."

I was in no temper for chitchat. Nevertheless, civilities prevailed. "Thank you for speaking to us, Dr. Jensen."

"It's Heidi." She squeaked as much as spoke, in a little-girl voice that suited her pink flowered top. "It's awful about Nicole and, like I told Tory, I'm worried about Piper. If I can help, sure, I'll do whatever."

"Okay for me to resume recording this?" My sister-in-law's finger hovered over a key.

"Sure."

As she activated the program and raced through the basics of who-when-where, I nearly levitated out of my seat with impatience. Once she was ready to roll, Tory began with, "Now that you've had a chance to think it over, do you have any surmise about where Piper might have gone?"

"I wish I did."

"Other old friends? A vacation cabin?"

"As far as I'm aware, she didn't keep in touch with anyone but me, and that was sporadic," the woman said. "If her family had a cabin, I never heard about it."

Questions tangled and tripped in my brain. I plucked out the one uppermost in my curiosity. "Did Piper ever refer to an Aunt Bonnie or Bernice? Or did you meet someone by that name?"

Heidi's forehead wrinkled. Despite living in a sun-drenched climate, she had only a faint tan. But then, as a dermatologist, she probably bathed in sunscreen. "I don't think so."

Tory tossed in a few more inquiries, which netted zero insights. But then, the two of them had covered a lot of territory earlier.

"How well did you know Nicole?" I interjected.

"I met her a few times. She was vibrant. Full of life." The face on the screen regarded us wide-eyed. "I can't believe someone murdered her."

"What about her daughter?" I pressed. "Did you meet her?"

"Little Wendy? What a cutie!" Heidi said. "Yes, once or twice. Piper was nuts about her niece."

So much for Piper's claim to be ignorant of her sister's pregnancy.

"Were the sisters close?" Tory asked.

"I wouldn't say they were buddy-buddy. There was maybe a little resentment on both sides."

"How so?" Not having any siblings, I hadn't considered that there might be tension in their relationship.

"Nicole shouldered most of the burden of caring for their mother while she was undergoing cancer treatment, and I suppose she resented that a bit," said the woman on the screen. "As for Piper, she got upset about her sister's drinking. And their mother's, too, although I only met their mom briefly. I'm relying on what Piper told me."

"Sounds like you were well acquainted with her family," I prompted.

"Not all that well. Everything filtered through Piper. She and I roomed together through college, med school, and residencies, although we have different specialties." Words poured out, with no indication of holding back or calculation.

"When was the last time you saw Nicole?" Tory asked.

"I think it was before their mom died, around nine years ago," Heidi said. "Then a few months later, Nicole disappeared."

"Taking Wendy with her?" Tory queried.

"That's right." She leaned back on the couch, her head nearly brushing the louvered window behind her. "Piper was worried, but annoyed, too. Her sister was always kind of flaky."

"Unlike Piper?" I couldn't resist sniping.

Heidi's grin revealed large teeth. "Yeah, she's emotional. I had to calm her down on a regular basis, especially after Nicole took a powder."

"How'd you do that?" Tory asked.

"I told her their mom might have been the only reason Nicole had stayed in Alaska. Once her caretaking was finished, she relished the freedom to travel or whatever." The smile froze. "That made sense to me then. I had no clue she'd been killed."

"Nobody did, until this week." Tory explained how they'd detected her body under a parking lot.

Heidi shuddered. "What about Wendy? Is she okay?"

"We're trying to find out." I considered asking if there'd been any discussion of who the father was, but nailing down the girl's whereabouts was more important. "It's possible Nicole left her with someone. Any sense of who that might have been?"

"None, I'm afraid."

My sister-in-law glanced at her notes. "Was she close to any cousins?"

I wished I'd brought that up sooner. Mentally, I thanked Tory's efficiency.

"Not that I recall."

"What about someone whose name sounded like Bernie?" I asked. "Or Bonnie or Bernice, as I mentioned before."

"Like I told you, I didn't know anyone... Oh. Wait." During her pause, I had an irrational impulse to reach into the screen and shake out her memories. "Wow, I completely forgot! She has a cousin Marnie. That might be a nickname."

My breath caught. Had we just identified a key player in this deadly drama?

"Marnie?" Tory repeated. "What's her last name?"

Heidi glanced off screen, as if at a noise. No baby wail ensued, however. I was grateful when her attention returned to us. "I think it's Smith."

"Maiden or married name?" Tory probed.

"Married. I don't recall her maiden name, if I ever knew it. Just this whole messy business about her marrying a guy named Bob Smith."

"Bob Smith?" I repeated. That had to be one of the most common names in the phone book, if anybody still issued phone books. And while the name Marnie was unusual, her legal name could be Maureen, Marianne, or something else. "Any middle name or other data that might identify him?"

She shrugged. "I'm not even sure if his name was Bob or Robert."

Tory cast me a back-off-Eric stare. "Just share whatever you remember."

Heidi nodded tolerantly. Considering how late the hour was and how cranky we must sound, she seemed very good-natured. That accounted for how she'd survived rooming with a high-strung woman like Piper. "The Blanchard sisters were supposed to be bridesmaids at their wedding. Wow, this was a long time ago. I mean, Nicole was pregnant then."

"Twelve years ago?" Tory added to her notes. Building a timeline, I surmised

"Yeah. It was June, everybody's favorite month for weddings, right?"

Much as I appreciated Heidi's cheery attitude, I wished she'd speed this up. "What do you mean, supposed to be bridesmaids?"

She drew in a long breath, searching for events from the

distant past. "You should understand, Bob didn't have much family. Maybe not any family. Marnie met him on a church mission, repairing an orphanage in Mexico. Anyway, before the wedding, which was in—hmm—I think it was in Idaho, like maybe Boise."

I don't give a damn where the wedding was! I bit down on the protest.

Tory gripped her pen hard enough to snap a lesser instrument. "Did something go wrong?"

Heidi re-boarded her train of thought. "He decided to come clean and bare his soul, or his past. He admitted to Marnie that he'd been married before and had a conviction for spousal abuse."

I got a sick feeling. We'd just uncovered an association between a violent man and Nicole.

Bob had served in the military in Afghanistan, Heidi said. Suffering from PTSD, he'd blown it when he returned home and his wife demanded a divorce. Furious when she informed him that she'd met someone else, he'd hit her. She'd suffered a black eye, and he'd pleaded guilty to domestic violence.

"He got probation with court-ordered therapy," Heidi wrapped up. "He swore to Marnie that he would never raise a hand against a woman again. Her parents insisted she cancel the wedding, which they were paying for."

"She married him anyway?" Tory's toneless voice didn't fool me. She was seething.

"They eloped." Heidi covered a yawn with her hand. "Excuse me. I don't think Piper saw them after that, but I'll bet Nicole stayed in touch. She was closer to Marnie. I think they were about the same age."

"Where are the Smiths now?" I asked.

"I'm not sure. Somewhere in Idaho, maybe."

Bob or Robert Smith might live in Idaho. Even in the age of

the Internet, that didn't mean we could identify him, although his criminal record might help us track him down. Still, I reminded myself, there was at best a tenuous link between him and the Blanchards. He and his wife might have nothing to do with Piper or Wendy.

Heidi was yawning again. "Is it okay to provide your contact info to the police?" Tory asked.

"Yeah, sure. If it helps keep Piper safe."

"When was the last time you saw her?" I asked. "In person, I mean."

"My wedding, two years ago in Seattle. She was my maid of honor." Tears glistened in Heidi's eyes. "Neither of us likes social media, but I should have tried harder to keep tabs on her. I mean, even with a husband and a baby, that's no excuse for my dropping the ball. If Piper had trusted me enough to confide about Nicole's murder, maybe she wouldn't have gone missing."

"Don't blame yourself," I said. "She might not be acting rationally."

"If you think of anything more, please contact me." Tory's hand hovered above the keyboard, as if about to end the session.

"I, um, I will. I really wish I could help. I just...well..."

The hesitation in Heidi's voice triggered an alert in me. I leaned forward. "What's on the tip of your tongue?"

"Oh, it's silly." A dismissive wave of the hand.

"Nothing's silly," my sister-in-law said.

"The reason, or one of the reasons, Marnie went ahead and married the guy was because she was pregnant," Heidi said. "I'd forgotten that. She had a little girl just a few months after Nicole did. And..." She stopped.

I was practically vibrating. "Please continue."

"It's funny. She called her daughter Wanda."

I got a prickling sensation, as if this must mean something. "Why such a similar name to Wendy?"

Heidi spread her hands. "Marnie and Nicole must have both liked the same name and agreed on variations. I've known families to do that."

If Nicole had decided to leave Wendy with anyone, it might well have been this cousin. There'd be a little girl about the same age with almost the same name, like a twin, an instant friend and companion.

But what about the aunt figure that Gus-the-grizzled in Juneau had cited? Where did she fit in? And what about the abusive husband?

Someone had been manipulating Piper, feeding her misinformation, casting me as the villain. I'd assumed this person was seeking Wendy, and maybe they had been. Had Wendy been staying with the Smiths? If so, what had they done with her?

I'd run out of speculations that weren't too terrible to consider. Mostly, I was afraid for the little girl who might be my daughter.

CHAPTER SIXTEEN

During my residency, I'd developed the ability to drop into a deep sleep and stay there. However, Heidi's revelations about Bob Smith and the questions they raised about Wendy's safety penetrated my dreams to the point that insomnia would have been a relief.

I awakened on Thursday with vague, dark wisps fleeting through my brain. Although they vanished, as dreams do, I half expected to receive bad news that morning.

There was, mercifully, nothing to compare to my painful awakening the previous day, when Keely had told me of Starla's murder. By contrast, I took a leisurely shower, then went downstairs for breakfast.

Morris and I shared the newspaper over bran muffins and fruit. He let me have first crack at the comics, while Tory downed assorted pastries, skimmed her phone and muttered about her plan to relay Heidi's comments to the police.

"I hate to think her name might wind up being blared over the Internet," she grumbled as she polished off an apple turnover. "Heidi's a new mom. She deserves privacy."

"As does everyone." Her father traded sections with me.

The news article on the front page simply recapped what

we already knew or suspected about Starla's death. Evidence from the car was under investigation. Witnesses were being questioned. The coroner's report was pending.

Between surgeries that morning, I checked for updates, but encountered none. For once, I wished Soraya would be more aggressive in her pursuit of the truth.

On my phone, I skimmed the hospital's email newsletter. A meeting, not mandatory but recommended, was scheduled for 11:30 a.m. regarding a festival to be held on Saturday. A hint about security concerns persuaded me to stop by.

The wood-paneled auditorium had a steeply raked floor, with great sightlines, not that there was much to see on the stage today. Just a large projection of a poster advertising the event, the Octoberfest Fair, featuring twin half-masks, one white and one black. I suppose that was to indicate that costumes were welcome.

"I'm only here because the kids insist on going," Nora said as she slipped into place beside me on the top tier. Below, about half the seats were occupied.

"Neo and Fiona?" I recalled those two appealing characters from her Labor Day party.

"My son's become Fi's faithful sidekick, not that I object." My colleague smiled. "They've been working on their outfits all week."

"Your husband didn't mention a security issue?"

"Leo's been working such long hours, he barely has time to say hello."

I reread the notice in my phone. "The hospital will be offering free flu shots at the fair. I don't see what the threat is. A feared attack by rampaging anti-vaxxers?"

Ignoring my attempt at humor, Nora indicated the stage below. "We're about to find out."

Our powerfully built administrator, Mark Rayburn, had

entered with a paler-than-ever Trent Horner. As Mark regarded us solemnly, the murmurings hushed.

"We're grateful to have Detective Horner of the Safe Harbor Police Department here to advise us about this coming weekend's events," he intoned. "With Sunset Park only a block away, we're expecting overflow parking in our structure. We're also concerned that you may encounter strangers wandering around the hospital. I'll let our guest explain."

Polite applause greeted Trent as he reached the microphone. "Thank you, Dr. Rayburn." His gaze swept the room. "I'm sure you've all heard about the recent tragic events in our city. Due to publicity, we're expecting a large attendance. Unfortunately, some people consider crimes to be a sort of game, where they can snoop for clues."

Among them were staff members at this institution, I reflected. Sadly, that inclination may have had tragic consequences for Starla.

"The ability to disguise themselves at the fair adds to the risk of attracting unstable individuals," Trent went on. "We value your alertness, here at the medical center or at the park, for suspicious behavior. If you believe there is imminent danger, call 911. Otherwise, please contact the regular police number." He provided it. "Any questions?"

"Why would people snoop at the medical center?" asked a man I couldn't identify. "The murders didn't happen here."

"Dr. Piper Blanchard, who remains missing, has admitting privileges," Trent said. "And other doctors have appeared in newscasts. People these days tend to think of everything and everyone as part of a TV reality show."

I appreciated his not naming me when he cited "other doctors." As if everyone didn't already assume who he was referring to.

"But what's the connection between the murders and the

fair, besides location?" persisted the questioner. Some medical personnel, being scientists, tend to be literal minded.

"Well, it involves prominent local figures." Trent hesitated as if debating whether to be more specific.

Beside me, Nora spoke up and filled in the blanks. "Reese Kendall is co-sponsoring the festival. I believe his wife has a face-painting booth."

The detective yielded the point. "That's right. Mr. Kendall was instrumental in the recovery of murder victim Nicole Blanchard's body."

"Which he brings up on the news every chance he gets," hooted Dr. Paige Brennan, Nora's office partner, from two rows below us. Chuckles rippled through the auditorium.

Trent leveled her a look that, from a more impressive figure, might have been daunting. "He has dedicated the festival to the memory of Starla Randolph, who worked here, as I'm sure you're aware."

The mirth died.

Mark reclaimed the mic. "Thanks for coming, everyone. We'll have extra security at the hospital, but there's no substitute for dozens of eyes and ears."

Trent nodded agreement.

Around us, people were rising. "I wonder why Trent's handling public information duty," I observed to Nora. "He may have to step back from the inquiry, but he's still a detective, right?"

"The regular P.I.O. is on paternity leave." Nora waited with me for a gap in the stream of audience members. "Trent must have been asked to step in today."

"Or he craves a reason to stay involved with the case," I hazarded.

"That's possible, too."

I should have moved faster. My dawdling left an opening for

the detective to reach us. "Dr. Darcy." He spoke in a low voice, and I squelched the temptation to rush off as if I hadn't heard. No doubt he'd only speak louder and attract everyone's attention.

"Yes, detective?"

We proceeded with Nora toward the hallway. "Might I suggest you stay clear of the park on Saturday? You're rather recognizable these days."

"Happy to avoid the lookie-loos." Family-oriented events aren't exactly my favorite pastime, anyway. "Is it true Starla was spying on me on your behalf?"

No guilty start. No telltale blush. "Absolutely not. But I'd certainly like to catch whoever she *was* snooping for."

"She told the press it was someone close to the investigation."

"Close in what sense?"

"Who knows?" In the corridor, I turned left. With a wave, Nora headed in the other direction.

Trent paced alongside me. "Might have been bravado. Let's face it, Starla enjoyed the spotlight." After a beat, he added, "That's not a criticism."

"I didn't think it was."

At the cafeteria entrance, I considered telling the guy to buzz off. Walking in with a cop—other than Keith, not that he dropped by often—would only intensify the rumor mill. On the other hand, if Trent stayed close, it would allow me to continue delving into whatever he might have learned.

It was a tossup, whether he would annoy the lab coat off me by prying or whether I'd be the one to sniff out data. Worth the risk, I decided.

With the scent of roast chicken as a lure, we both joined the hot-food line. To my irritation, the tanklike shape of Yvonne Worth inserted itself across the thin plastic shield from us.

"Officer Horner, how are you?" Her red-rimmed eyes peered at him. "We both miss her terribly, don't we?"

How much of her distress was due to her friend's death and how much to losing her partner in gossip? I wondered. Also, how much to missing her convenient ride around town?

"Yes. Yes." Distractedly, Trent indicated his choices from the food bins.

Although I was ahead of him, she'd served him first. Fine by me. The serving lady she'd displaced scooted over to assist me. Pointing at my selections, I kept my ears tuned to the discussion next to us.

"I can't believe she's gone!" Ms. Worth selected a large piece of chicken. "I hardly slept a wink last night." A dollop of potatoes au gratin crowded the plate. "Any progress in catching this monster?" A big serving of broccoli landed on top.

"I actually wanted the green beans," Trent said.

"Sorry."

"Never mind." He mustered a slight smile. "Broccoli's fine."

As we trooped to the cashier, I half-expected the nosy woman to shove into that position as well. Mercifully, the cafeteria supervisor was scowling at Yvonne, which short-circuited any further bulldozing.

With my uninvited companion, I joined Jeremiah at a table. Rod was absent; I'd learned from another anesthesiologist during the morning's surgeries that he was taking a few days off. His daughters were understandably upset about the murder of a woman who'd been staying at their home.

"What are you doing here?" Jeremiah demanded of Trent. The uncharacteristic hostility reminded me that my friend had undergone extensive questioning by Trent and Leo after Piper's flight, no doubt including the nasty insinuation that he and I had conspired to kill Nicole.

"Police business on the premises," the detective replied.

Jeremiah wasn't accepting a brush-off that easily. "What kind of police business?"

Since Trent was drinking his iced tea, I answered for him. "At the staff meeting, he warned us that the festival on Saturday might draw amateur crime solvers, and that they may show up at the hospital."

"Then why is he still here?"

Trent swallowed his mouthful. "Although I'm no longer involved in the investigation, I was close to Starla, and I'd appreciate everyone's cooperation. If you notice anything pertinent, please alert Sergeant Franco."

After processing this suggestion, Jeremiah said, more mildly, "Even under normal circumstances, I do not believe it is wise to hold a public festival where adults may disguise their identities."

"Agreed." The detective salted and peppered his food liberally.

I considered it my turn to grill him. "Have they received any indication where Piper might be?"

"As you're aware, I no longer have an inside track." He picked at his chicken. "What about you?"

Share a little, get a little back, I hoped. "Tory talked to Dr. Blanchard's ex-roommate last night, as I'm sure she's informed your colleagues. There's a cousin, possibly in Idaho, who might be in touch with her. Heard any reference to Idaho? Or a Bob or Marnie Smith?"

He shook his head. Stonewalling, or truly out of the loop, I couldn't tell.

Jeremiah was concentrating on his slice of apple pie. But also listening closely, I was sure.

"Speaking of relatives, how much do you know about Starla's cousin?" Trent angled his chin toward Keely, who was eating with her officemates, including Nora and Paige. Despite her grief, she'd resumed her duties today.

Was that why he'd stuck around for lunch, to pick my brain about Keely? I should have expected as much. "She's always struck me as honest and reliable."

"She cleans your house, doesn't she?" Without pausing, since the answer was obvious, he asked, "If she needs money, why not take on extra nursing jobs?"

"She's choosy about who she works for." I stopped there.

"What have you heard about her background?"

Rather than waste my breath arguing that he could look that up for himself, I ran through the bare facts. "Keely's worked at the hospital for more than twenty years. Dr. Brennan, whom she assists, speaks very highly of her. She does an excellent job on my house, as well."

"How did she and Starla get along?"

"I suppose there was some friction."

With a fork, he pushed aside his broccoli to get at the potatoes. "Did Keely resent having a younger, prettier cousin?"

"Not that I observed." To steer him off that unfair course, I added, "The first time I met Starla, in the space of about five minutes, she insulted my late wife's decorating and offended my father-in-law's catering assistant. Considering that, I'd say Keely was quite patient with her."

By now, the subject of our conversation had noticed the looks Trent was casting in her direction. Rising, Keely marched between the tables, heading toward us. I braced for him to receive a dose of her caustic bluntness.

"Since you're here," she began.

Trent stiffened. "Yes?"

Around us, conversations quieted. From Keely's table, the two doctors and her fellow nurses watched intently.

She clasped her hands in front of her, childlike. "I was talking to Starla's parents in Utah about funeral arrangements.

They said something odd."

Trent frowned. "What was that?"

"Well, they were asking about her life here. Whether she'd been running wild and that was what put her in harm's way. They wondered if she'd settled down since the last time she lived away from home." Keely drew a shuddering breath. "I had to admit, I wasn't able to keep as close an eye on her as I'd have liked."

Trent took out a notepad. "What kind of trouble had she been in before?"

"Drinking and partying," Keely said. "Here's the strange part. I asked where she'd lived previously."

"And?"

"She worked at a restaurant in Alaska." She swallowed. "In Juneau. Nine years ago."

CHAPTER SEVENTEEN

A connection between Starla and Alaska? Ramifications and implications rushed at me. Who would have suspected that chatterbox of harboring secrets?

"While she was in Alaska, did she meet Nicole Blanchard?" Trent asked.

"I'm not sure, but the restaurant where she worked was named Blanchard's," Keely said. "Unless she started her job after Nicole left, they must have run into each other."

Starla had known my former lover. Possibly she'd met Nicole's sister as well, although, if my mental chronology was reliable, Piper had been living in Seattle at that point.

That critical year had stretched from the cancer death of Mrs. Blanchard to Nicole's departure and slaying. The number of players in that scenario now included our latest victim, Starla. And, most likely, her killer.

"Why didn't you report this immediately?" Trent demanded.

"I am reporting it immediately."

They glared at each other. At Keely's table, Paige shifted as if to rise. Planning to stick up for her nurse, perhaps.

Jeremiah broke the tension. "It is curious that Starla did not confide in you, detective."

Unless she had, of course, and Trent was putting up a false front. While he didn't seem slick enough to pull that off, you could never tell.

Trent's belligerent expression shaded into a pout. "She should have. I don't understand it."

Paige eased down. But kept a watch on us, should she be needed. I appreciated her protectiveness toward Keely.

"Starla joked about that once," I recalled.

"About working in Juneau?" Trent's voice rose half an octave.

"About wishing she was a witness so you'd interrogate her," I said. "Then she giggled and added that she was glad she wasn't, because you wouldn't be able to date a witness."

"She withheld evidence because she was afraid I'd break up with her?" Frustrated, he smacked his thigh.

"It's unfortunate." While I hadn't been a fan of Starla's, it upset me to see her life snuffed out. "If she'd told you what she knew or suspected..." I didn't have to provide the tag line: *She might still be alive.*

"As they say on cop shows, she knew too much," Jeremiah summarized. "Perhaps she recognized the killer and he decided to silence her."

"Or maybe he saw the video where she said she knew more than she was telling," I put in.

Trent shot to his feet. "You need to come down to the station," he told Keely.

"I'm working."

"This is important!"

"So are my patients," she said. "Besides, I've told you everything."

Grimly, he put in a call to someone. Keely returned to her

coworkers, while Jeremiah and I finished our meal.

Other detectives would soon arrive to question Keely, I assumed, and wondered how Nora would feel when her office became part of her husband's investigation. About as happy as I'd been when Tory showed up at mine, I guessed.

The thought of my sister-in-law reminded me to contact her about Starla's Alaska link. "I'll see if I can get hold of Gus," she announced when I was done. "Maybe he remembers Starla and who she hung out with."

Gus? Oh, yes, the grizzled fellow. "You're sure he isn't the killer?"

"I'm not sure of anything," Tory said. "Except that I haven't seen the old dude hanging around Safe Harbor."

I dropped that far-fetched line of suspicion. "Granted, it's more likely she got to be friends with a young coworker. She couldn't have been more than twenty or twenty-one. And impressionable."

"Depends on how sheltered she was," Tory scoffed. "Kids can be pretty arrogant."

"I'm sure you run into that, in your profession," I said. "A doctor sees the other side, the naïveté." I'd treated too many young women stumbling through emotional and physical wreckage. *He said he loved me... I can't believe he lied...*

Had Starla and Piper both been manipulated by the same person? Whoever it was, he or she must have relocated here to Safe Harbor, to have maneuvered them so skillfully.

Since Starla had been killed yesterday, that meant he'd been here that recently. And if the goal was to find Wendy, it remained unaccomplished. But who was left for him to target?

Me, if the murderer believed I had information about my possible daughter. Damn, I wished I did know her whereabouts so I could protect her. In view of the killer's ruthless pursuit of his goal, however, it was an open question whether I could even protect myself.

"I do not believe it is wise to hold a public festival where adults may disguise their identities." Jeremiah's statement echoed in my head. Although I could avoid Saturday's festival, the park lay only a block from the hospital, where I had surgeries scheduled.

There'd be extra security. All the same, we were dealing with a practiced and presumably sociopathic trickster.

At my office that afternoon, I squeezed in two patients who were new to my practice and had to delay several other such requests. "You're a popular guy," commented Isaiah, who'd removed his white lab coat and was about to depart for a golf game. "Several of my patients have asked if I think you're a murderer."

I paused in the hallway between exam rooms. "Why would that make me popular?"

"People love celebrities." With a mock salute, my partner headed out.

Fame had never appealed to me, much less notoriety. But the case was undeniably fascinating.

Later that day, I checked my phone and discovered a new image on social media. It showed Piper entering the passenger side of a battered pickup truck in a Las Vegas parking lot.

She was in the background of a selfie, behind a young woman with a blackhead on her nose. It had taken a week for the photographer to recognize the news value of her shot.

The image didn't reveal the truck's driver, and only about the right-hand third of the grimy license plate. It had a red strip at the top with the letter O, a white center bearing a couple of numbers, and a dark blue, ragged bottom strip with the word "toes" in white.

I slotted in the missing text: "Idaho" and its motto, "Famous Potatoes."

Someone with Idaho plates had collected Piper. Had they met by design? Had they then returned to Idaho, or driven elsewhere? Was the driver Bob or Marnie Smith?

With luck, the police could combine this with the background Heidi had provided, and perhaps locate Piper. However, the whole picture remained as incomplete as that selfie, with many missing parts.

Nothing more hit the media for the rest of the day. At dinner, I kept my phone on the table, as did Keith, who'd joined Tory, Morris and me. Salmon and veggie burgers had been on the catering menu, along with a brown-rice medley and asparagus with mock-cheese sauce. Not Keith's usual repast, but he had better sense than to complain.

He'd run into Tory at the police department. Since both were annoyed at being out of the loop on the investigation, they'd gravitated to each other.

We reviewed the recent developments, plus my speculation that someone fixated on Wendy might turn his sights to me. "Unless that's pure ego on my part," I said. "I raise this possibility to forestall either of you pointing it out." Clearly, "either of you" excluded my father-in-law, a kindly man who tended to see the best in people and was always distressed when he encountered darkness instead.

"I'm forced to agree with you." Keith took a break from shoveling down food. "You and Tory may both be in danger."

"Why Tory?" Morris asked.

"Yeah, why me? I'm a bit player," my sister-in-law commented.

"You work for Eric," Keith reminded her.

"She does?" Morris's salt-and-pepper eyebrows drew a furry line.

"He hired her to snoop for him." Keith piled trimmings atop his salmon burger.

"That's not right." My father-in-law regarded his daughter. "Eric shouldn't have to pay you."

"Just reimbursed my expenses to Alaska, that's all." Tory patted her father's hand.

"Okay." He bestowed his approval thoughtfully. "As long as you aren't charging him."

"Because she gets free rent?" Keith asked before chomping into his mile-high sandwich.

"Because he's family."

Over the burger, his eyes rolled. Keith's not the sentimental type.

I glanced at the news/weather app on my phone. The forecast showed sunny and clear, no surprise for Southern California in early October. Nothing more about Piper. "All quiet on the Blanchard front."

"Don't be too sure." Keith finished downing his food. "If this guy Bob Smith is the killer, he's got his hands on Dr. Blanchard."

That prospect was unsettling. Yet it appeared from the video that she'd gone willingly with whoever was driving the truck. And while I considered Smith a prime suspect, that didn't tie up all the loose ends. "We haven't connected him to Starla's murder."

"He had several days to dump a body and drive back here," Keith pointed out.

"But why bother?" I asked. "He'd already made a clean getaway."

Keith shrugged off my doubts. "He's a convicted wife beater. Any perceived threat could have driven him to violence."

"Even if the truck does belong to Bob Smith, he admitted his past to his fiancée before the wedding, and got court-ordered treatment." Tory was, presumably, playing devil's advocate, since I doubted she had any sympathy for the guy.

"You're taking his side?" Keith challenged.

"I'm saying we shouldn't focus on him to the exclusion of everyone else."

"Once an abuser, always an abuser," grumbled my friend.

"Is that true, Eric?" Morris asked.

I don't consider myself an expert on the subject, except that it does arise with patients. A doctor may notice signs such as hidden bruises, cigarette burns, and poorly explained broken bones. While friends and relatives may not grasp the whole picture, it's hard to deceive your medical practitioner. Let's face it, how often does an otherwise healthy person fall down the stairs or run into a door?

It's a tough problem to address, since patients often refuse to disclose abuse, nor does domestic violence necessarily fit the assumption of male on female. It can be the other way around, or male on male—as my brother-in-law, a urologist, has mentioned—or female on female.

"There are a lot of factors that feed into violent behavior, like learned attitudes, personality disorders, a sense of entitlement," I said. "But I have to admit, with serious abusers, statistics indicate only a small percentage change their behavior long-term."

"But some do?" Morris asked.

"It's possible, if they're highly motivated," I conceded. "Keith, you've dealt with this stuff. What do you think?" As a detective in crimes against persons, he must have seen plenty of cases. And had a different perspective from mine, since I dealt almost exclusively with the victims, many of whom fervently believed that happiness rather than a clenched fist lay right around the corner.

He mulled it over before responding. "I'd have said, lock up the bastards. But the fact is, I knew a cop who got fired for hitting his wife. The guy was absolutely determined to turn his life around and stop acting like his father. Got into one of those intervention programs, learned to manage his anger, and stopped blaming other people for his behavior."

"Did it work?" Morris asked.

"Depends on what you mean." Keith was analyzing this in more depth than I'd have expected from him. "Did he save his marriage? No. But he's on good terms with his ex-wife, shares custody of the kids, and remarried. Happily, I've heard."

"Maybe Bob Smith straightened himself out, too," my sister-in-law said. "On the other hand, he has a criminal history."

"Well, do you or don't you believe in redemption?" her father asked.

"I suppose it happens," she said. "Still, most of the time, abusers are like cheaters. Once a..." She broke off at the storm clouds on Keith's face.

Until that moment, I hadn't realized how strongly I'd hoped for a reconciliation between these two people close to me. They had a lot in common, a lot to offer each other. But violations of trust cast a long shadow. His sexual exploits had humiliated and hurt her, beyond anything he'd considered when he was impulsively hooking up with a nurse in an on-call room.

"You'll never get over it, will you?" His tone was low, tight, and final.

Regret shaded Tory's expression. "Seems like I can't."

Morris and I moved to the counter to dish up the gluten-free carrot cake and provide the illusion of privacy. However, rather than talking, the former couple focused on their phone readouts. Catching up on messages, or news, or any excuse to avoid communicating. Perhaps there was nothing left to communicate.

"I'd love for my daughter to find happiness with the right

guy;" my father-in-law murmured, "but I'm beginning to wonder if she's a right-guy type of person."

I wasn't entirely sure what he meant. However, the reality, to me, was that in the past year, Keith had changed and matured. Tory might have changed, too, but not necessarily in the same direction.

"What the bloody hell?" Keith roared.

Startled, I peered at Tory. She was staring at her phone, just like Keith. "What?" I raced over to grab mine.

On the local news, Reese Kendall was blabbing away to his wholly owned reporter, Soraya. Not unusual, since he never missed an opportunity to thrust himself into public view.

"Is this about the festival?" He was sponsoring it, I recalled.

"Keep listening," Tory muttered.

"...been in the works for years," he was saying. "This is as much a merger as an acquisition, because I consider SnowState Devices to be in many ways a partner. We intend to retain the management, and there are no plans for layoffs."

"They'll keep their headquarters in Juneau?" the reporter asked.

"Absolutely." The man's bright blue eyes shone with pride, or greed, or something I couldn't put a name to.

"Juneau?" I repeated, startled by this association between Nicole's hometown and a prominent figure here in Safe Harbor. Rich entrepreneur, former mayor, Nora's ex-husband. The man who'd paid for the excavation of Nicole's remains, thereby inserting himself into the case.

Years ago, had he gone to Juneau on business and met her at the restaurant her family owned? Had he had an affair with her and felt threatened when she showed up in Safe Harbor nine years ago?

She might have she called him after I let her down. Had he manipulated her into meeting him, and strangled her?

"...an increasing demand for medical technology and, therefore, for the components manufactured by SnowState...." He went on talking.

With his expensive tailored suit and smooth confidence, Reese was a man Piper and Starla would have trusted. And he was running Saturday's festival, where his wife would have a face-painting booth. That set the stage perfectly for whatever the hell he was planning.

I could hardly breathe.

CHAPTER EIGHTEEN

What evidence did we have? Not much, if anything, just vague suspicions and coincidences, according to Keith. Nevertheless, he put in a call to his sergeant to make sure he'd learned of the newly revealed link between Reese Kendall and Nicole's hometown.

"Leo says he'll talk to him," he said after hanging up. "Discreetly."

"Reese has been sticking his nose into this at every step." Despite being aware that I was grasping at straws, I kept hoping some crumb of actual fact would emerge. "Like paying to unearth Nicole's body. And siccing his reporter on everyone connected to the case."

"As if Soraya needed encouragement," Tory said dryly. "But I'll check out his past, his whereabouts when Starla was killed, and so on."

"Why should he dig up Nicole's body if he placed it there?" Keith retorted. "He bought the property. He could have left the parking lot undisturbed."

I had no answer. Just instincts screaming that a killer this calculating, and with so much to lose, might have motives we hadn't yet grasped.

My theory of Nicole's daughter as a target didn't fit the picture, as far as I knew. But I couldn't expect all the pieces to slam together in an instant.

The approach of the festival in the park, now only a day and a half away, weighed on me. After another night of restless dreams, I awoke with the conviction that I had to take action.

In my experience, people tend to trust me with information, and while Leo had more access to his own wife than I did, he wasn't likely to bring her into the investigation without good reason. I had no such qualms.

In response to my text about meeting this morning, Nora replied that she planned to be in her office early. Catching up after yesterday's disruption, she said. While texts don't necessarily tell you much about the sender's state of mind, I gathered she wasn't happy about Keely being interviewed on the premises.

If I recalled correctly, Nora had still been married to Reese nine years ago. Presumably she'd already have informed Leo had she noticed any correlation between recent crimes and events of nearly a decade past. There might not have been much. A husband who traveled and cheated—well, since Reese had later slept with his executive assistant, to whom he was now married, that was a reasonable surmise.

That didn't mean he'd murdered his lover if she'd showed up in Safe Harbor. Still, I'd completely forgotten about Nicole's phone call to me the night of her disappearance, until Piper reminded me. Who could tell what details might lie buried in Nora's memory?

The medical building was unlocked when I arrived shortly after eight, but the ground-floor pharmacy was closed and the lobby empty. After mounting the stairs to the second floor, I swung toward Nora's office.

The door to the staff hallway stood ajar. That struck me as

odd. Usually doctors, nurses and techs are careful to shut it, to discourage patients from using the wrong entrance.

I stepped cautiously into a corridor almost identical to the one in my office. Near the end, through an open doorway, boomed a masculine voice I recognized from the newscasts.

"You've gone too far this time!" thundered Reese Kendall. "You trashed my reelection as mayor by spreading slurs about my supposed lack of family values. Now that I'm prepping a run for congress, you've got your husband demanding to question me in a murder case. You won't get away with this!"

"I have no idea why Leo asked you to stop by." Nora's tone was controlled but edged with concern, as any woman would be when confronted by a furious male. "You don't even know what he wants yet. You said so yourself."

"Obviously, it's related to my business dealings in Alaska and that murder case he's too incompetent to solve. As if I had anything to do with how a couple of bimbos wound up dead," the man snarled. "Stop harassing me, Nora, or you'll regret it."

I took out my phone, activated the video recorder, and moved forward. While I wished I'd done it earlier, Reese couldn't tell when I'd started, could he?

"Threatening your ex-wife?" I held up the cell as I stepped into view. "Not what I'd expect from a man of your stature."

Intense blue eyes glared at me with an ugly meanness that made me wonder how Nora could ever have married him. In person, he wasn't especially large—no taller than me—but from the muscles bunched around his shoulders and chest, I assumed he could land a mean punch. Or wring a woman's neck with ease.

His attention fixed on my phone. "This is a private conversation. You can't play that on the air." With a sneer, he added, "As if anyone would trust anything you claimed to have captured, Dr. Darcy."

As far as I recalled, we'd never been introduced. However, he could hardly have avoided recognizing me, with his news organization blaring my alleged involvement in Nicole's death.

Nor had I forgotten that I might be his next target, assuming it was he who'd written that note on Piper's windshield. But on this occasion, I had him at the disadvantage.

"My goal isn't publicity, I assure you," I said. "But I'd be curious to see how Sergeant Franco would interpret your remarks, should any harm come to his wife."

Behind him, Nora cast me a grateful look. With her pink blouse open at the throat and her blond hair pulling loose from its knot, she seemed especially vulnerable today.

Kendall's fists tightened and then relaxed. "I'm not a violent man. As Nora can attest. I never raised a hand to her during our marriage."

She shrugged. "Factually true." Her word choice implied he'd been verbally abusive. "Reese, I assure you, I have nothing to do with Leo's investigation. You're being paranoid."

The man glanced from her to me, or, rather, to my phone. Whatever he might have been tempted to hurl at her, he refrained. "Just clearing up a few private matters with my ex-wife. Stay out of this, Darcy."

"Gladly." I moved aside to let him pass.

His nostrils flared at this unaccustomed dismissal. However, Reese Kendall departed without further protest. Ah, the power of one tiny video recorder.

Nora mouthed the words, "Thank you." We waited to speak again until the hall door closed and I visually confirmed he'd gone. Only then did I stop the video.

Taking her white lab coat from its hook, Nora gestured me to a chair. Her private office had the usual framed certificates on the walls, along with a cute photo of her, Leo and their little boy on the desk. "Do you plan to show that to Leo?" she asked.

"Unfortunately, I didn't think to turn it on until after I heard him threaten you," I admitted.

"You were bluffing? Brilliant." A smile lit up her face as she drew on the coat. "Honestly, I never spread rumors about him. I didn't have to. His actions speak for themselves."

"Do you think he's a murderer?" I asked.

"He can be ruthless." She adjusted her collar. "I was never physically afraid of him during our marriage, though. He'd have to feel seriously threatened, and to believe he could get away with it, before he'd kill someone."

"When did you two divorce?"

"Seven years ago."

"Did you ever see or hear anything troubling around the time Nicole was killed, two years before that? A late-night phone call that upset him, for instance?"

"Not that I recall. He kept a lot of things private." Nora sighed. "In retrospect, he never let me get close to him, not really. Did he play around? Not that I noticed, until he started working ridiculously long hours with his new executive assistant."

That would be Persia, now a purveyor of fancy beauty products. I retrained my line of thought. "Did he travel to Alaska often?"

She considered. "I don't remember him mentioning it. Or that company, what's it called—SnowStuff?"

"It's a super long shot, but did you ever have any indication that Starla recognized him from when she lived in Juneau?" I probed.

"Starla Randolph? I barely knew who she was," Nora said. "I mean, she did stop by here once to say hi to Keely, and I saw her in the cafeteria, but that's it. I only learned her last name after she died."

Noises from the hallway disturbed our seclusion. Dr. Paige

Brennan peered in at us. "Is this about my nurse?" she asked. "Because I think she's endured enough."

Once again, I respected her readiness to defend Keely. Not that I enjoyed being glared at by a six-foot-tall woman with dramatic red hair and a truculent manner.

"No, it's about Eric saving me from my ex-husband's paranoia," Nora replied calmly. "I'll explain later."

"No offense." With a wave, Paige departed.

"Thanks for your time," I told Nora.

"Are you kidding? You were great."

I hesitated. "All the same, are you sure you want to take the kids to the festival tomorrow, with Reese around?"

She folded her arms. "Neo and Fi would be heartbroken if they couldn't wear their costumes. Besides, Leo's going with us."

"Be careful." Even a police sergeant wasn't Superman.

"Reese is too concerned with his image to do anything to me in public," she answered lightly.

Maybe so, but the raging man I'd seen fit her description of him as ruthless. I wasn't prepared to put anything past him.

On and off for the rest of the day, I worried about what might happen next. I even asked that the staff keep our private hall door locked, with the excuse of preventing access to reporters and other snoops. Despite the inconvenience of having to enter through the waiting room or text someone to admit them, they readily agreed.

We were all on edge. I didn't object to Glenda monitoring the Internet during lulls between patients.

She gleaned more from social media than from newscasts. Unfortunately, it was mostly vague and occasionally verged on the bizarre. Several trucks similar to the one Piper had entered had been sighted in a range of locations. One parked outside a Nevada brothel was identified as belonging to a televangelist, whose career was presumably about to suffer a major hit.

"Here's a weird story," Glenda announced during a quiet moment. "Somebody spotted a truck just like that, with Idaho plates and everything, and a couple of kids alone in the cab."

"Somebody left their children unattended?" Farrah scowled at this negligence.

"No, the kids were driving."

"Both of them?" I wondered if the joke had a punchline.

"Unclear," the receptionist chirped.

"How old were these kids?" my nurse asked.

"Too young to have a license," Glenda said.

"But big enough to reach the wheel and the gas pedal," I pointed out. "Where were they, exactly?"

Glenda checked her readout. "Heading south on US 93, between Boise and Las Vegas."

We all agreed it was unlikely Piper was returning to Vegas or, beyond that, to Southern California. And highly probable that the driver was simply so young-looking that someone had misidentified him or her as a child. Indeed, I wouldn't have been surprised if someone had reported seeing a penguin or Bigfoot at the wheel. That's the glory of social media.

When I finished work, daylight lingered outside, with clear, mild weather. Although Sunset Park lay in the opposite direction from my house, it was only a block out of the way and I decided to swing past.

Surrounded by neatly tended houses, the quadrangle sported palm trees, picnic tables and a playground. At this dinner hour, only a few children scrambled across the brightly colored fixtures.

Uniformed workers had begun setting up extra trash bins and portable toilets, as well as directional signs. A few vendors were erecting booths in the open grassy area, flanking lanes defined by small markers.

Near what appeared to be a main access, a striking, dark-haired woman in layers of flowing purple cloth stood with hands on hips, snapping orders at men setting up a bandstand near her booth. Through my open window, I heard her shrill voice declare, "To the left, you idiot! My left, not yours!"

That would be Persia Kendall, a familiar figure around town. This was the woman who'd helped wreck Nora's first marriage—ultimately doing my friend a favor, in my opinion—and whose store was replacing Delicious Memories, the gift shop and bakery built by Trent's parents. I considered it a loss for the community, but then, I'm not a consumer of skin-care products and essential oils.

I slowed to a halt along the curb. Since there was no traffic, I wasn't blocking anyone, but a sudden thump on the top of my car made my hands jerk on the wheel. Glancing up, I half-expected to see a police officer ordering me to move along.

"What the hell are you doing?" Reese Kendall demanded through my passenger window. "You have no business here."

"How do you know?" I retorted.

His thin mouth gaped briefly before he said, "I didn't see your name on any list of participants."

"It's a public park." For good measure, I added, "And street."

"Leave my wife alone." Was that a tinge of worry beneath the overbearing manner? Even if he was the murderer, he might still feel protective toward his current wife.

"I'm not bothering anyone," I told him.

"You're obstructing traffic. And I don't want to see you anywhere near this place tomorrow."

Reese knew as well as I did that he had no right to banish me from a public place. Although tempted to reply along the lines of Try-and-stop-me!, I held off. No sense engaging in a childish squabble.

Since an SUV had just pulled up behind me, I put my car in

gear and rolled forward. Reese, who'd kept one hand on my roof, jumped back. Thank goodness he didn't take a tumble. I'd have been obligated to stop and check on him.

Driving home, I wondered if he'd spent part of the day being grilled by Leo. That would certainly account for his foul mood. Too bad they hadn't arrested the jerk.

At home, I learned that Tory had contacted Gus. He vaguely remembered Starla and said she'd been friendly with everyone on the staff. He didn't recall ever meeting Bob or Marnie Smith, or Reese Kendall, either.

Although she'd been tied up with an insurance fraud case most of the day, Tory assured me she had put out feelers about the latest development concerning Reese. I responded with details of my unpleasant encounters with the aspiring congressman.

With several surgeries scheduled for the next morning, I was still debating at bedtime whether to show up at the festival. And decided to do it, if only to figuratively spit in Reese Kendall's arrogant face.

CHAPTER NINETEEN

"I hate to burst your bubble, but I did some digging last night," my sister-in-law said over breakfast.

"What bubble?" I muttered.

"It doesn't seem likely Kendall's our killer. For starters, SnowState Devices wasn't incorporated until seven years ago," Tory said. "No apparent reason for him to have visited Alaska before then."

I washed down my food with a swallow of coffee. "He might have gone up there to hunt or fish."

She didn't bother to contest that weak response. "Also, the night Starla was killed, Kendall attended a charity dinner. According to one of my sources, he left around eleven and drove home with his wife. Claims he went straight to bed."

That wasn't the most airtight alibi, since Persia could have dropped into a near-coma with the aid of sleeping pills, or lied. But the combination of discoveries kicked my reasons for suspecting Reese close to, if not directly into, the Lost Causes dustbin.

I still hated the guy. He'd threatened Nora and he'd thumped my car. More urgently, that left a killer unidentified and on the loose.

It had been a relief to believe I knew who to blame, and could therefore keep my eye on him. Since I feared I might be the next target, it was disturbing to know a blow could strike out of anywhere, from anyone. At the hospital, at the park, in my car.

While driving to the hospital, I ran through a mental list of remaining suspects. There was the unstable Piper and, of course, Trent, despite his seemingly genuine grief for Starla. The police might, at a guess, be focusing on Jeremiah or on me, or both, due to our old acquaintance with Nicole. Maybe on Keely, with her relationship to Starla, although she had no known ties to Nicole. None of us was the killer, in my opinion.

That left the mysterious Bob or Robert Smith, cousin-by-marriage to Piper and the presumed owner of the pickup truck with Idaho plates. He'd been acquainted with Nicole through his wife, Marnie, and they might well have been entrusted with a little girl named Wendy.

My daughter? She'd be twelve now, about the same age as aspiring medical examiner Fiona. How would I ever manage to protect her when I couldn't even pin down her location? But if she was with the Smiths, why would they leave threatening notes in an attempt to find her?

Speaking of young girls, my anesthesiologist friend Rod had plenty to say about his teen-age daughters that morning. Usually busy collecting gossip from the staff, today he grumbled aloud as he assisted me in performing a hysterectomy on a forty-four-year-old woman who suffered pain and bleeding from fibroids.

"I've never seen Tiffany and Amber so clingy and scared," he told me. "At fourteen and sixteen, they mostly act like miniature grownups. Today they begged off on the festival. Too jittery."

"They might be a little old to enjoy parading around in costumes," I remarked. "Except at a comics convention."

"My wife's upset, too," he went on. "Karen's been stewing about the notion that Starla might have brought the killer home with her."

That grabbed my attention. "She brought men to your house?"

"Not that I'm aware of, but Keely's suite has a separate entrance," he said. "It's unlikely, though. Keely wouldn't have tolerated her cousin messing about on the premises."

I understood how his daughters felt. Even in these seemingly safe surroundings, with extra security guards patrolling the halls, my skin prickled with a sense of impending danger. Operations require a lot of personnel, including scrub nurses, technicians and a circulating nurse, and not all of today's players were familiar to me. Or fully identifiable under their surgical masks.

Quit being paranoid. Examine this rationally.

In the back of my mind, as I worked, facts struggled to sort themselves into a narrative, now that we'd more or less ruled out Reese. Building on the assumption that Starla's murder was linked to Nicole's, the younger woman must have known something or recognized someone that caused her to become a threat. In view of the disclosure that she'd worked at the Blanchard family's restaurant in Alaska, perhaps it was someone she'd met there and re-encountered here.

Returning to my theory about an obsessive search for Nicole's child, this acquaintance could have fixated on Wendy. Nine years ago, Nicole became alarmed and fled, sharing her plans with almost no one, not even her sister.

She had, I now believed, planned to ask me for help, either out of friendship or because I was the girl's father. But en route, my former lover must have detoured to drop off her child in what she considered a safe place.

Whoever had tracked her to Southern California must have heard her mention me at some point, perhaps as the father, and checked the local motels. When they caught up with her, they'd strangled her in an attempt to force out the little girl's location. It seemed that Nicole had taken her daughter's secret to her shallow grave.

After that, everything appeared to have gone into a holding pattern. The child had vanished, possibly entrusted to the Smiths, whom the killer might not have known. Yet why wouldn't Marnie have reported Nicole missing when she never returned for her daughter? Why hadn't she contacted Piper over the years?

Don't get distracted. Keep following the thread.

Recently, somehow, Piper had reconnected with her cousin, according to what Piper had told me that first night at Jeremiah's. The cousin had related that Nicole was last seen heading to Safe Harbor to visit me, and had claimed she was in danger.

But not from me. Piper had gotten that part wrong. Still, this information had set in motion a sequence of events that had led to the unearthing of Nicole's body and, directly or indirectly, to Starla's murder.

While Piper was in town, she'd been manipulated by someone. Who? Who else might fit into this scenario? Marnie and Bob, whereabouts unknown; maybe grizzled old Gus—who remained in Alaska, where Tory had met him—and Starla.

Wait. There had been one other person in the picture, according to Gus. That was Bonnie or Bernie, the aunt-type friend of the elder Mrs. Blanchard.

No one fitting that description had surfaced. But, as I closed the surgical wound, my brain kept churning.

Starla's arrival in town might have occurred by chance, due

to discovering her DNA relationship with Keely. I didn't see how anyone could have manipulated that. So how had she fallen in with deadly company from her past?

Aside from Rod's household and Trent, only one other person had been close to Starla. "Secrets don't stay secrets forever," Starla had declared in front of a camera, and anyone could have seen it on the news site and felt threatened. But the person she'd said it to directly... no, that couldn't be. Too ridiculous. Too random.

Hold on... What had Piper claimed in the cafeteria, when she apologized about the initial gossip? That she'd foolishly disclosed too much about her sister and me to a casual acquaintance from her motel. Another person new in town.

I had wondered why she would shoot her mouth off to a stranger. But what if the woman she'd pointed out hadn't been a stranger?

And what if the name Gus had strained to recall wasn't Bonnie but Vonnie, a nickname for Yvonne?

For the second time in as many days, I felt as if I'd turned over a rock and come face-to-face with a rattlesnake. I searched for details to cast doubt. Instead, my narrative gained traction.

Yvonne and Starla had already been friends from when they both worked at Blanchard's. No wonder they'd hung out together, and Starla could have agreed to snoop on me at Yvonne's request.

But in a fatal twist, Starla must have recalled—or Yvonne believed she had—some key detail that tied the older woman to murder. A trip she'd taken nine years ago, an absence that coincided with Nicole's death?

Thank goodness my patient was ready for transport to the recovery room, because I could no longer concentrate on anything but my earth-shattering insight. Exactly what should I do about it? I had no proof, only suspicions.

"You've got the strangest expression on your face," Rod observed.

"It's Yvonne," I said.

"Who is?"

"The person who killed Starla and Nicole."

We stared at each other. "You just worked that out while you were operating?" He shook his head admiringly. "I knew there was a good reason I loathed that woman. Well? Why are you standing there?"

Since I don't bring my phone into the O.R., I hurried out to grab it. Who did I call first? Not 911; what emergency would I report?

Operating on instinct, I tried Keith, and got voice mail. "The killer is Yvonne Worth." Did he even know who that was? "She worked with Starla at the cafeteria."

Since I hadn't entered Leo's or Ed Hough's number in my phone, Tory came next. I blurted my conclusion.

She accepted it immediately. "Right under our noses. Any idea where she is?"

"Might be working." I hadn't stopped in at the cafeteria that morning.

"See if she's there. Don't confront her," Tory said. "I'll alert Leo and Ed. With luck, they can close in on her before anyone else gets hurt."

"Give me Leo's number, just in case." He was supposed to be a block away at the festival with Nora, their son and his friend, I recalled.

She provided it and ended the call.

After stripping off my surgical garb, I hurried down the stairs from the second floor, keenly aware that I might be about to face a cold-blooded killer. Despite Tory's warning, I had no doubt Ms. Worth would see the truth on my face. Did she carry a weapon? Even if not, she could grab a knife.

Breathing hard, I strode into the cafeteria. There was no hot-food service today, just sandwiches and packaged salads. The only person in a bright yellow uniform was a woman staffing the cash register.

"Where's Yvonne Worth?" I blurted.

She took a beat to register my question. "She went over to the festival."

"Why?" I could apologize for my rudeness later, if necessary. Although I didn't immediately grasp what harm Yvonne could do, the woman had free rein in a park full of unsuspecting children and visitors.

"Why is she at the festival?" the cashier repeated as a couple of technicians approached with their trays. "I'm sorry, I have to ring up this order."

"It's urgent." There was no time for explanations. "Please, what's she doing?"

The staffer accepted the newcomers' payment as she answered. "She said she was going to meet her daughter. That's strange because she told me once her daughter died a long time ago. What do you suppose she meant?"

I had no idea what went on in Yvonne's warped mind. And much as I wanted to warn this staffer and others about her, I couldn't risk having them tip her off. "Thanks for the info."

At Leo's number, I got his voice mail. I left a rushed but clear message, and tried Keith again. Same result. I texted him, for good measure.

Who next? 911 or Tory? Before I could nail down my move, my phone rang.

Caller unknown. Not some damn spammer! About to reject it, I noticed the place of origin.

McCall, Idaho.

I didn't know anyone in that entire state, and I had no idea where the town or city of McCall was. But the coincidence was startling enough that I answered. "Dr. Darcy."

"Eric! It's me, Piper!" As if I wouldn't recognize that sharp tone. "Wendy's in horrible danger and it's all my fault. I'm so stupid! I can't believe I didn't see through Yvonne. Yvonne Worth killed my sister!"

I wasted no energy on the irony of her turning to me, whom she'd done her best to paint as the villain. "Why aren't you calling the police?"

"I tried!" Piper sounded borderline hysterical. Not unusual for her. "The dispatcher thought I was some kind of nut case."

They must receive a lot of prank calls and false sightings. "Surely she offered to put you through to the desk officer."

"I couldn't wait on the line with Wendy in danger!"

"How is she in danger?" I had to penetrate Piper's out-of-control emotions. "Isn't she in—where are you, Idaho?"

"Yes. But..."

Her phone must have been on speaker, because I heard a man's voice next. "This is Bob Smith, Dr. Darcy. I'm married to Piper's cousin."

"Yes. Go ahead." Despite my mistrust, I needed a cooler head than Piper's to summarize this situation.

"Wendy and my ten-year-old son, Bob Junior, who thinks it's his job to protect her, are driving my truck to Safe Harbor," said the man. "They might even be there by now."

I remembered the news report about kids in a pickup with Idaho plates, heading in this direction. Not so wild a tale, after all. "Why?"

"They got some false information and thought I posed a threat." Was that regret, or bitterness, or simply anxiety in his voice? "We assumed they'd go to a friend's house and come home in a few hours. Instead, this Yvonne Worth tricked them into driving to your area to meet her."

"I'm the one who told them she was the only person we could trust!" Piper wailed. "Now we can't reach them. We saw on the news that Starla was murdered and that she'd lived in Alaska nine years ago. That's how we put it together, that it was Yvonne."

"Any idea where they're meeting her?"

"We don't know," Bob said. "I doubt she'd deliberately hurt Wendy, but she'll kill my son if he gets in her way."

"Please alert the police," Piper threw in. "They'll believe *you*."

"I have a pretty good idea where she is," I told them. "At a festival a block from the hospital. Got a photo of the kids you can send me? And what's your truck's license plate number?"

Bob took care of both items in a flash. I got off the line and called 911. Although the dispatcher promised to issue a BOLO—Be On The Lookout—and notify the detectives, I wasn't sure she grasped the immediacy of the danger.

A photo showed up on my screen, of two preteens with heads tipped together. The girl was a miniature of Nicole: long, golden hair, mischievous amber eyes. Was this the face of my daughter?

The boy had black hair and a square face. He might be only ten, but from the set of his jaw, he looked like he could hold his own in a fight. I hoped so.

I forwarded the photo to the dispatcher, and for good measure, added it to a quick alert to Tory, Keith and Leo. Would it do any good? Would it arrive in time?

About to head for my car, I realized that with the expected jam of visitor parking, it would be faster to run there on foot. It might be up to me to save Wendy and her little-boy protector.

I set out at a lope.

CHAPTER TWENTY

As I thudded along the sidewalk, my rhythm subconsciously conforming to the mariachi music blaring ahead, I struggled to figure out my next move. Locate Yvonne. No, spot the children who might be in danger. Wait. Find Leo or some other authority figure who could grasp the situation and rally the troops.

Vehicles of various sizes clogged the edges of the road. Pedestrians sashayed along the sidewalk, and I kept having to dodge them.

Unanswered questions taunted me. Why had Wendy believed she was in danger from Bob Smith, and was she wrong? With Piper's judgment notoriously questionable, why should I buy her story? And, as with that long-ago call from Nicole, how did I actually know where this one originated? Piper and Bob might be nearby, waiting to spring a trap for some murky reason.

Yet my conclusions pointed more strongly than ever to Yvonne as the killer. The clues seemed to tally.

The scents of grilling burgers and cinnamon-doused churros wafted on the breeze, while costumed kids popped out at each other, laughing and shrieking. More festival-goers crowded the sidewalk. A dangerous place for a confrontation.

At the green, I spotted a uniformed officer and was about to head toward her. Then I sighted another, larger figure farther off. Leo. I yelled his name and waved, but got drowned out by the music.

A woman turned. Nora had heard me, or sensed my arrival. Her eyes flew wide when she noticed my gesturing, and she gazed around frantically. I felt as if I could read her mind: Where were her son and his friend Fiona? A mother's primary concern.

Nowhere in sight. If I'd passed them, I hadn't recognized them in their costumes.

She grabbed Leo's arm, and his forehead creased as he, too, became aware of my agitation. Nearing them, I shouted, "Check your phone!"

He did. Saw the picture, the text, the warning. Wishing I'd copied it all to Nora, I blurted a few words to her.

And added one key detail: a description of Yvonne Worth. She had flown so far under the radar that, although she must have talked to the police about her "good friend" Starla's death, Leo might not even remember her.

He began barking orders into his phone. "We need to cut off the music!" Nora shouted. "And find the kids. I'll call them from the stage."

Which kids did she mean? All of them, I hoped as I hurried alongside her, helping cut through the festival-goers. If nothing else, the height of the stage should provide a decent view over the flat, grassy spread.

The closer we drew, the thicker the throng, partly because of its proximity to Persia's face-painting booth. A popular diversion, the kiosk spawned flocks of colorfully decorated kids of all ages.

Finally we broke through, only to encounter a man blocking

the platform steps. Reese Kendall's expression shaded into disgust when he spotted us.

"Stop the music!" Nora shouted. "We have to make an announcement."

Reese's lip curled. He didn't budge.

We should have brought Leo. Damn. "Children in danger!" I snapped.

"You're just trying to disrupt the event," he shot back.

"Lost kids!" Nora shrieked. "Stop the music! Give me the mic!"

Reese braced his legs and folded his arms. Unbelievable. I considered punching the jerk, but that might simply add another level of chaos.

Someone tugged at his shirt, a girl about Neo's age, her face striped like a tiger. "Daddy!" she cried. "Won't you help the lost kids?"

In his eyes, defiance warred with another emotion—maybe the desire to appear big in his daughter's eyes. After glaring at me, he jumped on the stage and waved the musicians to a halt.

Nora hurried up to take the mic. When I followed, I caught a glimmer of bright yellow on the edge of the park, well behind the platform. Yvonne, in her uniform.

"Hey!" I yelled at Nora, but she was facing away from me, preparing to speak. Taking out my phone, I pressed Leo's number. Voicemail. He must still be talking to someone. I left a message and skimmed down the steps.

People were clustering close to the stage. I thrust between them, heading toward Yvonne. Where had she disappeared to? There, near the sidewalk, close to a parked SUV.

Don't confront her. Good advice, had I not spotted two children sauntering in her direction, a familiar brown-haired girl wearing a red cape over a blue tunic, and a much shorter boy in a gray sleeveless shirt, carrying a plastic mallet.

Over the speaker, Nora said, "Neo Franco and Fiona Denny, please report to the stage immediately."

At the sound of their names, the pair swung around. But Yvonne stepped into their path. What the...?

Awareness hit me, that she couldn't identify one preteen girl from another. The youngster she remembered from nine years ago could easily have been this one. She might not even know the age of the boy accompanying Wendy, and didn't care.

"She'll kill my son if he gets in her way." I didn't doubt it.

She'd told the cashier that her daughter died a long time ago; had she seized on Wendy as a replacement? She'd strangled Nicole and, a few days ago, poor giddy Starla, and she wasn't about to let anyone stop her now.

She caught Fiona by the wrist and yanked her toward the vehicle. Startled, the girl lost her balance and stumbled.

I raced across the grass. "Stop!"

"Dr. Darcy!" Fiona screamed.

A group of oblivious teenagers forced me to break stride. With all these people around, why didn't someone else step forward? Since we were behind the stage, no one up there could see us, I comprehended as I heard Nora repeat her command for the children to report to the stage.

I broke through the pack of teens. "Yvonne, stop!"

Abruptly, a boy blocked my path. Black hair, square face, hard jaw. "You've done enough harm, Dr. Darcy!" he shouted at me. "Leave that poor woman alone."

A quick take told me this must be Bob Junior. Thanks to Piper, he believed me to be the enemy.

"Are you crazy?" Fiona screamed from beyond him. "Dr. Darcy's my friend!"

"Yvonne Worth is kidnapping the wrong girl," I snapped.

Startled, Bob swung to get a closer look at what was happening. Fiona writhed in the woman's powerful grip, while little Neo whacked Yvonne's leg with his plastic mallet. "What the hey?"

Pushing Bob aside, I ran forward. Only to see Yvonne produce a small knife from her pocket and hold it to Fiona's throat.

"This baby belongs to me!" she cried. "I've killed for her and I'll kill again. Nobody's taking her away from me, especially not you, Doc!"

"I don't understand." Bob arrived next to me. "Why's she doing this?"

"Yvonne's a murderer. She's been trying to frame me." I peered anxiously around for a blue uniform or any familiar figure who could help. Nothing but gaping costumed kids and confused parents. Surely someone in authority should notice us. If only we weren't behind the damn stage!

If I sent Bob to circle from one direction and I approached from another, we might catch the woman off guard. Or she might stab a ten-year-old boy who was playing hero, and kill Fiona into the bargain.

Her attempt to shuffle toward the vehicle hampered by her little assailant, Yvonne kicked at Neo. The six-year-old reacted by dropping the mallet and winding himself around her leg, hanging on tight. "Help help help!" he shrilled.

Crazy brave kid. His dad ought to be here. Where *was* Leo?

I didn't dare tackle Yvonne with her knife pressed to Fiona's throat. While I doubted she would murder the child she supposedly loved, I couldn't run that risk. "That isn't Wendy, it's Fiona Denny!" I shouted at her. "Let her go and escape while you can."

"You're lying, you bastard!" she fired back. "I know my own child!"

"She's crazy." Bob sounded shocked. Well, no wonder.

"Aunt Vonnie?" a girl's voice chimed in from my right, just

outside my peripheral vision. "What are you doing to that girl?"

It seemed to me that we all froze, although that couldn't literally have been true. I saw the tableau with sharp clarity: the graying woman, staring in disbelief at the twelve-year-old she'd spent nearly a decade seeking but didn't recognize; the two costumed children; the stunned young would-be protector standing helpless beside me; and especially the preteen newcomer who mirrored Nicole from the golden halo of hair to the wide amber eyes.

Either unable to grasp this latest setback or acting from sheer instinct, Yvonne resumed angling toward the SUV. She still held the knife alarmingly tight to Fiona's throat. One stumble, and there'd be blood everywhere. Too much blood.

Spreading my hands to indicate I was unarmed, I eased forward. "You've got the wrong girl. Please let her go."

Still clinging to her leg, Neo chose that moment to repeat his soprano squeak. "Help help help!"

"Release her. She's not Wendy," I repeated. A few of the growing knot of onlookers appeared to be dialing 911. Most were busy shooting video. "You can still escape."

Wendy, too, moved toward the deadly tableau in front of us. "I'll go with you, Aunt Vonnie. Just don't hurt that girl."

"No, Wendy." Bob Junior cried. "Can't you see she's nuts?"

"Sssh." She fluttered her fingers at him in a Stop gesture. "Aunt Vonnie, I promised to meet you here, didn't I? Don't hurt an innocent person."

Wendy was willing to risk her life for a stranger. I felt a burst of admiration, almost pride, except that I deserved no credit for her character.

"You aren't Wendy," Yvonne sneered. "Where's my little girl? Where's my Wen-Wen?"

"She's hurting me!" Fiona reached toward her neck, where a spot of blood had appeared. "Get this monster off me!"

When Yvonne's arm tightened, a primal instinct sent me plunging forward. Mercifully, the knife moved away from Fiona... and pointed at me.

The girl was wriggling. I had to keep her captor focused on me. "Is this what you've become, Yvonne?" I demanded. "Is this how you want Wendy to see you? As a monster?"

"You're the monster!" Fury reddened her skin. "You abandoned Nicole when she needed you. You practically killed her yourself!"

"But you were there for her, weren't you?" My tone low and soothing, I held her furious gaze while Fiona slipped away from the knife's edge.

"Damn right! I'm the one who took care of the baby, while she got drunk! When her mother died. I handled everything. The funeral. The restaurant. Then she robbed me of my child!"

"But Wendy's over here," I said. "Look at her. She's not a little kid any more."

"It's me," Wendy confirmed. "I'm Wen-Wen."

"No..."

With a duck and a twist, Fiona stumbled to freedom and Neo rolled onto the grass, clear of Yvonne. For a stunned moment, the loutish woman stared from one girl to the other, and then she charged straight at me.

I barely had time to raise my arms defensively. Around me, people scattered.

From out of nowhere, a figure came flying in a wild frizz of chestnut hair, knocking my assailant to her knees and then onto her stomach, and wrenching her arms behind her. "Anybody got cuffs?" Tory demanded as she put her weight onto her cursing subject.

As I kicked the dropped knife far from Yvonne, I discovered I was shaking. Swallowing hard, I regained control. I hadn't survived a deadly encounter only to collapse—on livestreaming video, too.

The cavalry arrived, in the form of Leo and Keith and a couple of uniformed officers. They soon had Yvonne trussed and the knife bagged as evidence, while Nora wrapped her arms around the children and examined Fiona's neck.

"It doesn't look deep but I'll bet it hurts like fire," she told the girl in the red and blue costume. "I'm sorry."

"It's not your fault." Fiona folded her arms like the tough character she was. "I shoulda kicked her in the guts. Neo, you were super."

Leo looked up from his phone, where I guessed he'd been canceling the alert. "What was that business with hanging onto her leg?" the sergeant asked.

"I saw that on YouTube," the little boy said. "Wasn't that cool, Daddy?"

"You were incredible." His father shook his head, torn between pride and, I presumed, a terrible awareness of his son's close brush with evil.

"What are you kids dressed as?" asked a woman, aiming her phone at the youngsters. "Supergirl and, uh...?"

"I'm Thor!" Neo snatched up his plastic mallet and waved it. Nora appeared torn between tears and laughter.

"I'm Dr. Strange, not Supergirl," Fiona corrected.

No doubt we would be subjected to this scene from multiple angles on every news and social media outlet known to humankind. I resolved to keep my electronic feed turned off for the next twenty-four hours.

"Thank you, Tory," I told my sister-in-law.

"All in a day's work, rescuing your butt." She grinned.

After what we'd just endured, it seemed odd but necessary to make introductions. I regarded the girl who stood with Bob Junior. "I'm Eric Darcy," I said. "This is my sister-in-law, Tory Golden."

"Are you my father?" Wendy asked.

Damn those video-shooting lookie-loos closing in on us. "That's what we need to find out," I said.

CHAPTER TWENTY-ONE

"I had no idea you even existed until Piper showed up," I told Wendy, shifting to shield her and keep my back toward the video lady.

"Well, I didn't know about you, either. I grew up thinking I was Wanda Smith." The girl tossed her long hair, a motion eerily reminiscent of Nicole. "And that Bob was my brother."

"Yeah, I was clueless, too," agreed her younger companion.

"What happened to the real Wanda?" Around us, I noticed officers collecting names and videos. Nora was on her phone to Fiona's parents.

"My sister died when she was three. I was only a year old," said Bob Junior. "She fell off a tire swing and smacked her head on a rock. Wendy was too young to understand and my parents didn't tell anybody."

"Why on earth not?" Tory batted away another onlooker's pesky phone and glared until the guy withdrew.

"You'd have to ask them," Wendy said.

Keith arrived to separate us. "We need everyone to stop talking until you've been interviewed at the station. Don't discuss what you've witnessed, with each other or anybody else."

"You on the case again?" Tory asked.

"I guess so, for now." His stern expression bordered on a scowl. "That is, if you're finished risking your neck for Eric."

"He was risking *his* neck for the kids," she pointed out.

"Yeah, he's a big hero."

I chose to ignore Keith's misplaced jealousy. "I'll drive myself to the P.D."

"Yeah, do that. And please don't talk to the press." Keith indicated Soraya and her camera operator, who'd beaten the rest of the media to the scene because they'd already been covering the festival.

As I watched, she thrust a mic at Leo, who waved her off. Immediately, Reese Kendall stepped in front of her and began speaking as if he'd been in the midst of the action the whole time. Since he was Soraya's boss, she could hardly object.

With no further conversation permitted, I relinquished Wendy and Bob Junior to Keith, and headed to the nearest pharmacy to buy a paternity test. Although my office can collect DNA samples for that purpose, this would be quicker.

The store was overflowing with people, many in costume from the festival, picking up sunscreen, aspirin and Band-Aids. Nobody appeared to pay me any attention.

Waiting in line for the cashier, I put in a call to reassure Piper that the kids were fine. She explained breathlessly that she'd been following events on social media, apologized for suspecting me, and assured me she'd be flying in on Sunday.

"Are your cousins coming?" I asked in a low voice, wary of eavesdroppers.

"No. They have a lot to sort out with the authorities here," she said. "Can Wendy and Bob Junior stay with you till I get there?"

I hadn't considered the logistics. "Sure, if I can clear it with the police." My daughter—maybe—would be staying at my house. Hard to wrap my head around that. "Why do the Smiths have a problem with the authorities?"

"An unreported death," Piper said. "Accidental, they swear, and I believe them. Although I wasn't so sure... that's a long story."

"Wanda's?"

"The kids must have filled you in." She went on talking. "Their daughter died in a fall from a swing, about six months after Nicole left."

"Why didn't they report it?"

"They were afraid police would blame Bob because he'd had a conviction for domestic abuse a long time ago. Marnie's a nurse, but when she couldn't revive her little girl, they buried her on their property. Since they'd promised Nicole to keep Wendy's presence a secret, they passed her off as Wanda all these years."

"What if Nicole had returned?"

"She'd been gone quite a while by then. But honestly, they must not have been thinking too clearly."

Piper would be the expert on that, from personal experience, I reflected as the line ahead of me edged forward. "Why on earth did Wendy and Bob Junior drive a truck from Idaho? They're nowhere near old enough." I wasn't sure whether this constituted breaking my promise to Keith not to discuss the case, but it didn't affect anything I'd witnessed.

"They learned to drive on the farm. As for why they ran away, it's part of that long story I'll tell you when I get there. But I have to stop by the Safe Harbor police department first. They insist."

I'd reached the counter. "Okay, Piper. I have to go."

"See you tomorrow."

After paying, I took the kit and myself to the station. Once I'd located Wendy and explained the situation to an officer, I obtained a cheek swab from her and added my own. I called the diagnostic lab in L.A., where the operator stated that, if the kit arrived by 8:30 a.m. the next day, results would be posted on a confidential site by 6 p.m.

My next move was to arrange for a service to deliver it. If the courier considered it odd to be picking up a medical package at a police station, she didn't comment.

One day to wait for the results. It seemed like forever.

Preparing to write a witness statement, I struggled to sort out everything that had happened. My fears of an attack at the hospital, followed by the discovery that Yvonne was the killer. The alert from Piper and Bob Senior about the children facing danger. My desperate race to the park, the frustration of trying to locate Leo and then Yvonne, and my encounter with Wendy.

Most of all, the shocking sight of the knife held to little Fiona's throat and the imminent threat to Neo, who hadn't had much of a clue about his own peril. Where had all the adults been? How had this come down to me and a quartet of kids confronting a knife-wielding maniac?

As I organized my thoughts, I gave thanks for my sometimes annoying, usually reliable, take-no-prisoners sister-in-law. If not for Tory... well, that didn't bear thinking about.

Tensely, I finished writing as many relevant details as I could recall. In an interview room, with the recording devices activated, Leo read over my statement, asked a few questions that prompted additional details, and held up an evidence bag. "Do you recognize this?"

I did. "It looks like my sports watch."

"Can you identify it for certain?" His crisp manner helped me focus.

"I have the registration number at home." I promised to text it to him, and also provided the password. "It's been deactivated, though."

He jotted a note. "When was the last time you saw it?"

"I discovered it missing last Saturday morning as I prepared to go for a run." I laid out the circumstances, including my belief that Starla might have taken it while cleaning the previous day.

"Did you report it stolen?"

"No, because of the possibility it had simply been misplaced. Where'd you find it?"

"In Ms. Worth's quarters."

As I'd suspected, the older woman had manipulated Keely's cousin. The excitable Starla must have enjoyed the thrill of being an insider, until her memories, coupled with her loose tongue, posed too great a threat.

"It's evidence. You may or may not get it back," Leo said. "And, Eric?"

"Yes?"

"I'm grateful to you for protecting the children. I can't thank you enough."

"They're great kids." I didn't want credit for simply taking action.

It was nearly dinnertime when detectives finished debriefing us. There was some uncertainty as to whether the youngsters could be handed over to me, but a phone conversation with Piper, as her aunt, and with Marnie Smith, as Bob Junior's mother, seemed to settle the matter for the moment.

I was glad two already traumatized children didn't have to stay at a county facility overnight. My motives, in fairness, were partly the belief that they'd fare better at my house, and partly curiosity. Not every answer had to be put on hold while I awaited Piper's arrival.

I didn't envy Keith. He and his colleagues would be tied up long into the night and over the next days, untangling two murders and an assault/kidnap attempt. Even though they had plenty of witnesses along with video evidence, including a partial confession from Yvonne, they'd be sifting through all the other millions of details that don't show up on TV cop shows.

Bob Junior didn't hesitate to climb into the front seat of my car, and plied me with questions about how the electric vehicle operated. Wendy sat quietly in the rear during the short jaunt to my house.

"Wow," she said when we turned into the driveway. "This is a mansion!"

"It's cool," Bob agreed.

Viewing it through their eyes, I felt both pride and gratitude for this three-story home, with its dark half-timbering in the Tudor revival style. "I grew up here." I refrained from noting that, depending on the DNA results, she might soon live here as well.

Too much to sort out. The twelve-year-old didn't need additional stress.

Tory's sedan was already in the garage. Good. She'd promised to rustle up a change of clothes for the kids, who'd fled with no belongings and slept in the truck last night.

When we entered, Wendy's eyes widened as she surveyed the high ceiling and the blue-green, pink and pearl hues of the décor. The lowering sun raised a delicate shimmer through the stained-glass window on the landing.

Starla had declared it bland. Nicole's daughter had no such lack of appreciation.

"It's the most beautiful building I've ever seen, except for the state capitol in Boise," she said.

"My late wife was an artist. She chose the colors."

"When did she die?" Bob Junior asked.

"Three years ago." The cut of grief never vanished, but it

had faded.

"What did she die of?" Wendy asked artlessly.

"Complications related to cancer." That was close enough to the truth.

My sister-in-law trotted down the stairs with a pile of clothing and tossed the garments onto a couch in the great room. "Anybody hungry?"

The kids nodded.

Tory and I whisked leftovers onto the counter, along with plates and tableware. The kids stared dubiously at the unfamiliar foods, from black rice to green tortilla-prosciutto mango wraps, to apple and chicken Caesar salad.

"Where's your sense of adventure?" Tory challenged the boy, who had wrinkled his nose.

"It's all healthy stuff," I added. "Eat up." Since my father-in-law was catering a large event tonight, I assumed we should clear space in the refrigerator for a new infusion of tasties.

"Yeah, let's not act like country bumpkins," Wendy told her brother and took a plate.

The kids nibbled, then dug in with hearty appetites. During breaks in chowing down, Wendy asked me about Nicole. Where and how had we met? What had she been like? How and why had we split up?

I answered honestly but kindly, stressing the contrast in our temperaments rather than my enduring love for Lydia. Tory listened without comment.

Once we were at the cake and ice cream stage, I decided to pose the question I'd put to Piper earlier. "Why did you two run away and drive here on your own?"

They exchanged glances across the table. "Yeah, the cops wanted to know that too," Bob Junior said.

Tory and I waited. Silence prompts people to speak, and it had that effect on Wendy.

"Well, Mom—Marnie—told Aunt Piper about how Wanda died, and Aunt Piper didn't believe it was really an accident. She thought Dad—Bob Senior—might have killed her and that Nicole found out and he'd killed her too." Wendy paused to draw a breath. "So my aunt grabbed the keys and we ran to the truck."

"Yeah, they had this big argument, Dad and Piper, about stealing his truck, and he hauled her out of the cab," Bob Junior put in. "I guess she hurt her ankle and she was screaming. When Wendy started the engine, I jumped in with her in case she needed help. And we kind of drove off."

"That must have been a noisy argument," Tory observed. "The neighbors didn't call the police?"

Wendy frowned. "What neighbors?"

"Oh, it's a farm, right?" Tory said.

"Not a big one." Bob Junior seemed more interested in the discussion than I'd have expected from a ten-year-old. "We grow crops and raise chickens and stuff. Dad makes metal sculpture and Mom works part-time as a nurse."

"She sews beautiful quilts, too," Wendy said. "She's teaching me."

"You're home schooled?" I asked.

"No. I mean teaching me quilting."

"Let's get back to how you ended up driving across two states to meet Yvonne," Tory said.

"Piper made me memorize her phone number, just in case." Wendy spoke with straightforward candor. "She said Yvonne was the only person we could trust."

"Guess she was wrong about that, huh?" Bob Junior put in.

"And I was the villain of the story," I contributed wryly.

"I'm sorry." Pink spread across Wendy's cheeks. "That wasn't fair."

"It's not your fault," I said. "So you guys called Yvonne?"

They'd used Wendy's for-emergencies-only cell phone. Yvonne had provided basic directions to Safe Harbor and the park, and promised to meet them there.

"When she described the festival, it sounded like fun." The boy swirled a spoon through his nearly melted ice cream.

"Then the phone conked out," Wendy said.

That accounted for why Piper and the Smiths hadn't been able to contact them, I thought.

"How'd you pay for gas?" Tory asked.

"Dad keeps money in the glove box." Bob Junior sighed. "Man, he's going to be ticked off."

"I imagine he's thrilled you're safe," I said.

He spooned the last of the ice cream into his mouth. "I should call home, huh?"

"Let's clean up first," Wendy said. "You stink."

"So do you!"

"Not as much, 'cause I'm a girl. We don't sweat, we glow."

In a flash, they'd become kids instead of players in a deadly drama. Aside from the need to testify later at Yvonne's trial, with luck they could put all this in the past.

Tory, who'd raided both our closets, provided them with sleep shirts, plus T-shirts and shorts for the next day. After exclaiming over the fact that there were multiple bathrooms to choose from, the kids took luxurious long showers.

His hair still wet, Bob sat in the den with Wendy beside him and phoned home. He put it on speaker, allowing me to introduce myself to Marnie Smith.

Piper had departed with a family friend on the two-hour drive to the Boise airport. Bob Senior was still being questioned by McCall police but hadn't been arrested, as far as his wife knew.

"He insisted on keeping Wanda's death a secret, even though I'm the one who saw her fall. He wasn't even close by."

She spoke fast. "We both showed terrible judgment, but Bob wasn't just worried for his own sake. Nicole had said she and her daughter were in danger, and since she hadn't returned and we didn't know what happened to her, we figured we'd better go on keeping Wendy's presence a secret. She was only three, so it wasn't hard to pass her off as Wanda."

"Did Nicole say she was afraid of me?" I asked.

"No. She'd received death threats, but she wasn't sure who they were from," she said. "At one point, Nicole nearly left Wendy with an old friend in Juneau until whatever danger passed, but she decided whoever was after her might try to use her daughter as a hostage."

I had a pretty good idea who that "old friend" had been, and where the threats had originated. Also, who had poisoned Piper's and Starla's minds against me. "Did she say she planned to contact me?"

"Not by name. She did say Wendy's father might be willing to help her."

A wave of pain blurred my vision. If only Nicole had asked me, I'd gladly have helped. And she'd called me Wendy's father. Speaking of fathers... "Is there anything we can do for your husband?"

"Piper promised to pay for the lawyer we hired," Marnie said. "According to him, it's only a misdemeanor to fail to report a death, unless you're attempting to hide—how did he put it?—the manner of death. We *want* the police to know the manner of death, because it was accidental."

"I'm sorry for running away, Mom," Bob Junior said. "We didn't smash up the truck or anything."

"We're not mad," his mother said. "You were being brave. How's Wendy?"

"I'm here," she said. "I'm worried about Daddy."

Daddy. How long before that became me rather than Bob

Senior—if ever?

After the call ended, Wendy stared sadly at her brother. "I almost wish I'd never seen that picture of the upside-down trees."

"What upside-down trees?" Tory asked.

"That's how this whole thing started, me remembering stuff from Alaska and us getting in touch with Aunt Piper." The girl yawned. "I'm wiped out. Is it okay if I explain tomorrow?"

"Of course." I cut off Tory's attempt at a protest. Our curiosity could wait.

We got them settled, Wendy in the spare bedroom and Bob Junior on the couch in the den. Hearing Morris arrive, Tory went downstairs to update him.

Recalled to duty, I texted the registration number of my sports watch to Leo so he could identify it. Since I preferred not to watch the news, I turned in early.

Tomorrow, I would learn about the upside-down trees from Wendy and fill in more blanks from Piper. And manage somehow to endure the hours until the lab posted its results.

CHAPTER TWENTY-TWO

Out of habit, I arose early. After checking that the kids were still asleep, I went quietly downstairs and helped myself to coffee, which had brewed on a timer.

With no one else stirring, I sat at the kitchen table and clicked my laptop to the local news site. A couple of jerky amateur clips showed a knife-wielding Yvonne confronting me and being tackled by a furious Tory. They didn't include any shots of Fiona or Neo.

Perhaps Leo had insisted on that, or the powers that be—the media—had suffered an unusual spasm of good judgment. Reese did, after all, have a daughter about Fiona's age.

A sharper image captured Soraya in front of the police station, dressed as usual in a stylish suit and heels. The reporter's bleary eyes and the clear early light indicated this had been shot today.

I increased the volume. Briefly, she recapped Saturday's events: the assault and attempted kidnapping of a child, followed by the arrest of hospital cafeteria worker Yvonne Worth as a suspect in two murders. Since I already knew this stuff, I listened idly while mulling the merits of eating something from the fridge or waiting for my father-in-law to fix his traditional Sunday morning waffles.

"According to police in Juneau, Alaska, Ms. Worth maintained an apartment there outfitted with toys and furnishings suitable for a preschooler," Soraya said. "*The Safe Harbor Journal* has confirmed that Ms. Worth had bought plane tickets to Juneau in her name and that of Wendy Blanchard, the daughter of murder victim Nicole Blanchard."

After a pause while Soraya listened to something the audience couldn't hear, she said, "I've just learned that Yvonne Worth had a conviction in Juneau thirty years ago for negligence in the death of her year-old baby. She was accused of leaving the girl in her car while she was drinking in a bar. It appears she served a short stint in prison."

That might explain the fixation on Wendy as a replacement. Had Yvonne imagined the child was in danger due to Nicole's drinking, or was that beside the point? Some things might never be revealed unless the woman chose to confess.

That included how she'd tracked Nicole to Safe Harbor. Somewhere along the line, I supposed Nicole must have mentioned my name, along with my hometown. Since there were only a couple of local motels, that might have been enough to get her killed.

A beep announced a text from Piper. "Landed safe. En route to P.D. Kids ok?"

I texted, "Yes. Good luck."

"Not looking forward to this." She signed off.

The detectives would have a lot of questions and, based on my experience, they would cover the same ground repeatedly, from different angles. Could take hours.

The kids trooped down the stairs, outfitted in oversize T-shirts and shorts secured with belts. Tory must have shared a hairbrush, because I glimpsed a few reddish strands among Wendy's blond ones.

My father-in-law, wearing striped pajamas, emerged from his downstairs bedroom on the far side of the great room. "Hi, I'm Morris," he told them. "Tory's dad."

After I introduced the kids, Morris set to work with his waffle maker. Joining us, Tory took in the scene at a glance. "You couldn't have gotten a head start on the waffles?" she grumped at me.

I sprang to my own defense. "Last time, you complained about the lumps."

"Not to mention that you burned them, which is really hard to do, with that automatic buzzer." Tory poured herself a giant-size mug of coffee.

"You make my point." I grinned. "What do you kids usually eat for breakfast?"

"Fresh eggs," Bob said.

"Apple or berry muffins." Wendy tucked a napkin onto her lap.

"Sounds great. I'll have to visit the Smiths sometime," I said. "By the way, Piper's in town and headed for the police department. She's being grilled as we speak, and not for breakfast, either."

The kids chuckled. Even Tory cracked a smile. The prospect of her disagreeable client being roasted must have amused her.

While we waited for waffles, Wendy explained yesterday's comment about the trees. "My friend Amy and her family took a cruise to Alaska. She was showing me her pictures, and there was this scene that looked amazingly familiar."

"Of what?" Morris asked from the counter.

"They call them Flower Towers. They're upside-down trees with flowers and stuff planted in the roots." A glow lit her eyes. "They're at this place—what is it?"

"Glacier Gardens Rainforest." Bob Junior positioned the syrup bottle close to his plate. "It's near Juneau."

I tapped the name into my phone, and there they were, just as described. Flower baskets in midair, where there should be branches and leaves.

"Yeah, there's this funny story about a guy shoring up the area after a landslide and stuff kept going wrong." Wendy moved the butter near her, a countermeasure to her brother's bogarding the syrup. "He got so frustrated that he used his big equipment to yank up a tree by the root ball, flip it and slam it down."

"That sounds satisfying," Tory observed. "How're the waffles coming?"

"The kids get the first batch," her father answered. "You and Eric can wait."

"No hurry." To my embarrassment, my stomach growled. "Go on about the tree."

"Instead of smashing, it stuck in the mud, upside-down," Wendy said. "The guy decided it kind of resembled one of those flower baskets, if you trimmed the roots and added some mesh."

"He planted flowers in it?" Morris poured batter into the waffle maker.

"Yeah, with soil and moss and whatever. And it occurred to him he could recycle a bunch of upended trees, not just one," Wendy went on. "They're gorgeous."

"Don't the flowers die?" Tory asked. "I mean, it freezes up there."

"I guess they replant them every year," Wendy said.

Okay, enough botany. "How did this result in your contacting Piper?"

"Like I said, I remembered those trees," Wendy told us. "And a woman, holding my hand as we stared up at them."

"What woman?" Tory probed.

"Mommy," Wendy whispered.

That gave me a chill. Wendy might have been only three years old when Nicole died, but she hadn't forgotten her mother. Not entirely.

"When Wanda—I mean, Wendy—told our parents, they got real quiet," Bob Junior put in. "Then they went in the other room and argued. I heard my mom say they couldn't keep it secret forever."

"They came back and admitted I wasn't their daughter. Dad—Bob Senior—didn't look happy." Wendy sighed. "Talk about weird! There was this whole story about how I was actually from Alaska."

"They told us my real sister died, but not how," Bob Junior added.

Tory fidgeted, either from hunger or curiosity. "Did your father ever act violent? Did he hit you or your mother?"

Both children shook their heads. "He has a temper," Wendy said, "but he takes it out on his metal sculpture."

Bob Junior broke in happily. "Yay! Waffles!"

Morris set plates in front of them, and for a few minutes quiet reigned as they ate.

I broke the silence. "Why did they contact Piper?"

Wendy swallowed some milk. "In case she knew where Mommy was. She didn't, but she said Nicole would never have left me so long, that something bad must have happened to her."

"How did my name come up?" That seemed to me a key point.

"Piper told us she'd met you in Boston and you might be my father," Wendy said. "She thought Mommy might have been coming to see you."

"And that I'd killed her?"

"Something like that," Bob Junior said.

"Nicole did phone me, right before she disappeared," I

conceded. "But she didn't mention being in danger."

"Why not?" Wendy asked.

"When I told her I was getting married the next day, she must have decided not to confide in me." It was important that Wendy believed me. "I had no idea she'd had a child. She wished me luck and that was that. I didn't even know she'd gone missing until a few weeks ago, when your aunt showed up."

The girl stared at her empty plate before responding. "After Aunt Piper talked to my parents, she called somebody. She didn't mention me, because she'd promised to keep it secret about me being there. But after she got off the phone, that's when she brought up you and Safe Harbor."

"This person she called, was it Yvonne?" I had a pretty good idea.

"Vonnie," Wendy murmured. "That's the name she used."

"That was the only person she thought she could rely on," Bob Junior said. "I mean, except my parents, I guess."

"Some grownups don't have a lot of sense," Tory observed.

"That's for sure," Morris agreed, and brought another round of waffles.

After breakfast, Tory and Bob Junior went to the den to play videogames. Wendy expressed interest in the rose garden she'd seen through the rear window, and I was happy to provide a tour.

"My mother planted these," I told her as we strolled along a bark-strewn path. Mild October sunshine bathed the yard in gentle warmth. Not a big yard, by Idaho standards, I supposed, but with the surrounding stucco walls and leafy plantings, it had a secluded air. "Each type of bush has a name."

"Like what?" She stopped to smell a dark red blossom, one hand holding her hair away from the thorns..

"That one's Mr. Lincoln." I fished more from memory.

"There are bushes called Love and Honor and Cherish." I pointed to a stunning bloom with a bright cream center surrounded by strawberry-red petals. "That's Double Delight."

She sniffed it. "Wow!"

"Your grandmother... my mother would have enjoyed seeing you here," I said.

"Is she still alive?" Inquisitive brown eyes shifted toward me.

"She died when I was thirteen, of cancer." I had to cough to clear my throat.

"You lost your mom, too."

"That's right." I'd still had my father, though. "Did the Smiths treat you well?"

A smile chased away her air of sadness. "They're great." A frown followed. "I hope they're okay. They were just protecting me."

"If they did nothing seriously wrong, their lawyer should get it sorted out." I hoped that was true.

Hearing a stir in the house, we went in. Piper was standing beside Tory in the great room. How strange to see her again, the woman who'd tormented me for weeks.

The gray eyes no longer froze me out; relaxed muscle tone had replaced the rigid body language. She'd traded her blood-red lipstick for a softer shade.

Piper approached me as if for a hug, then thought the better of it and shook hands. "I already apologized to Jeremiah for everything I put him through, but you got hurt the most. I'm sorry."

I couldn't bring myself to forgive her, not yet. "How'd the interview go?"

"Kind of like a colonoscopy." Hugging Wendy, she spoke over the girl's shoulder. "Without the sedative."

Although it was only three-thirty, I checked my email for

the promised link, in case the lab posted early. No such luck. "I'm expecting the results of a paternity test," I explained.

"Good," Piper said.

Sitting beside her aunt, Wendy twisted her hands together. "If you really are my dad, would I have to... I mean, would I live here?"

"I'd like that," I said. "But let's not worry about it now." There'd be a lot of adjustments, well worth it. For me and ultimately, I believed, for her.

"The children explained about the upside-down trees and how the Smiths contacted you," I said. "Why did you reach out to Yvonne?"

"I was frantic. She was an old family friend and I thought she might remember something useful." Piper shuddered. "It never occurred to me she could have killed my sister."

"You stayed in touch with Ms. Worth over the years?" Tory asked.

"She called me every now and then. She always asked if I'd learned anything about Nicole or my niece. It didn't seem suspicious."

Wendy spoke up. "You said you hired a detective to find Mommy, right?"

"I did, after she'd been gone a while," Piper confirmed. "When he struck out, I imagined she'd met some guy and changed her name, or moved to another country. But she'd never have abandoned you. When the Smiths told me she'd left you with them, I got this awful, sick feeling.."

"What did you tell Yvonne about Wendy?" I asked.

"Well, I'd promised the Smiths not to mention her. After all, if someone had been threatening Nicole, he might still be around." Piper cupped her niece's hand with hers. "I made up a story about an anonymous phone call claiming my sister was dead. I figured that if Nicole had shared any secrets with

Vonnie, that might jolt her into telling me."

"It jolted her into something, all right," Tory muttered.

"She immediately mentioned Eric as a suspect, and it struck me as credible." Piper blushed. "I was such an idiot."

Tory and I exchanged glances. No argument there.

"I'd already been planning to relocate, after breaking up with my boyfriend," Piper said. "I recalled a posting about the position at Chuck's office in Safe Harbor."

"And you brought Vonnie along, for good measure?" I didn't restrain an edge of sarcasm.

"No! It shocked me when I discovered she'd moved here, too," Piper said. "She claimed she was here to support me. She made it sound perfectly reasonable."

"You never doubted that I was the bad guy in all this?"

"After the jerk I'd dated, I guess I was easy prey to believe the worst about men." Piper tilted her head apologetically. "She painted you as an arrogant rich doctor who'd dumped my sister and then, when she asked for help, killed her."

"He isn't like that," Wendy reproved. "You should have seen him standing up to that nasty woman!"

"She tried to stab him," Bob Junior added.

"Tory was the hero. Heroine," I said.

My sister-in-law rolled her eyes. Not big on flattery.

"I saw the video clips. I'm sorry for putting you all in danger. And for letting Vonnie manipulate me." Piper sighed. "Poor Starla. I never met her in Juneau and I only ran into her at the cafeteria a few times, but we had something in common. We both fell for Vonnie's lies."

"At least you had the sense to run off," I said.

Tory started another eye roll but caught herself.

"Honestly, I was terrified of you," Piper said. "I arranged for Bob to pick me up in Vegas. He was really decent about it. Then I freaked out when Marnie told me how Wanda died. I assumed

Bob was the killer."

Poor judgment must run in their family, I thought. Nicole, Piper, and perhaps their cousin as well.

Periodically, I checked my email. At 5:48, I recognized the lab's name as the sender and clicked. There it was, the link to the private site that might change my life and Wendy's forever.

My throat tight with fear and longing, I clicked on the link.

CHAPTER TWENTY-THREE

Cold, hard numbers, charts, and a conclusion: I was excluded as Wendy's father.

Excluded. Zero percent possibility.

It had to be a mistake. We should run this again. Submit an official, witnessed, chain-of-custody paternity test that would bear both our names, instead of identifying numbers, and be admissible in court.

To what end? It would simply prolong the agony. This was a reputable lab. I didn't believe it would have made such a huge error.

"Eric?" Tory's voice reminded me that others were waiting.

"It's negative." In case the children didn't understand, I clarified, "I'm not Wendy's father."

"Then who is?" she asked.

I had to smile through the hurt. "They don't tell you that."

A memory drifted to the surface. Shortly before our affair, Nicole had broken up with a law student. Was it possible they'd remained friends with benefits while she was dating me? However, that slim recollection would be more likely to torment than help Wendy, since I didn't know the man's name or even which law school he'd attended.

"I think Nicole assumed it was you." Piper glanced at me sympathetically.

"How does that work?" Bob Junior asked. "Was she married to somebody else?"

No, she just slept around. That would be cruel, and unnecessary. "It's complicated." I left it at that.

Until a few weeks ago, I hadn't known Wendy existed. Why, then, did regret and longing grip me? Why this dark sense of loss?

Wendy's lips pressed into a straight line. Hard to read her mood.

"It's too bad," Bob Junior said. "I could have visited here. We'd go to the beach and Disneyland." The theme park lay half an hour's drive up the freeway.

"Maybe one of those DNA ancestry tests could identify my father," Wendy said. "People find relatives that way, don't they?"

"They aren't always happy with the results." Tory's comment reminded me of Keely and Starla.

"I'd wait on that," Piper agreed. "At least till the dust settles."

"Oh, my gosh." Wendy stared at her. "Where will I live? Can I go back to the Smiths?"

"You can stay with me as long as you like," Piper said.

I had no comment, as this ball was no longer in my court. Speaking of court.... "You should hire a family attorney to straighten this out," I said. "The sooner the better."

"Got a recommendation?"

I suggested a firm one of our doctors had used when adopting her nephew.

"I'll get right on it," Piper said. "If the lawyer says it's okay, I'll take the kids to Idaho and sort things out there. Seriously, I'm happy to provide a home my niece." She patted the girl's hand.

"You'll return our truck?" Bob Junior asked. "Dad will be really mad at me if you don't."

"Hopefully, yes," Piper said.

"Will I be able to live near the Smiths?" The girl who wasn't my daughter spoke thoughtfully. When would I stop wishing this bright, brave youngster belonged to me?

"I'll rent a motel room in McCall." Piper took out her phone. "Later on, I'd like to join a practice in Boise. It's only a few hours away."

"But the Smiths are my family," Wendy protested. "I've got friends in McCall. And I already missed too much school."

Piper tapped a link. "I won't fight for custody, not if you don't want me to. But ultimately, a judge is going to decide about that, anyway." She left unspoken that much would depend on whether the Smiths were cleared in Wanda's death.

I nearly suggested keeping in touch with me as well. A warning glance from Tory stopped me. Neither Wendy nor Piper nor the Smiths had any real connection to me. Not any longer.

The next day, I took a break from seeing patients to say goodbye at the Harbor Suites, where Piper had stayed overnight. She planned to return in a few months or whenever Yvonne's trial began, she said, but the kids—both itching to get on the road—probably wouldn't be needed.

After a few hugs, they piled into the pickup truck. I watched them drive off, Bob Junior's elbow poking out the passenger window and, in the center of the front seat, Wendy's blond hair floating until it seemed to merge with her aunt's.

She didn't look back.

It was only as I drove away myself that it occurred to me that these past weeks had changed me. Without being aware of it, I'd moved on without my wife, investing in the future, even though this particular wished-for future hadn't materialized.

I pictured the trees in the Alaskan rainforest. Yanked out by the roots and slammed upside-down in the mud, then planted with flowers, they'd been transformed.

There must be an appropriate metaphor lingering there. I didn't have time to dwell on it, though, because I'd arrived at the medical center, and people needed me.

THE END

ABOUT THE AUTHOR

A former Associated Press reporter and TV columnist, *USA Today* bestselling author Jacqueline Diamond has sold more than one hundred novels. These include mysteries, medical romances, Regency romances and romantic comedies published by Harlequin, St. Martin's Press, William Morrow and Five Star Mysteries, among others. Jackie and her husband live in Southern California.

Jackie is best known for her Safe Harbor Medical romances and mysteries. Among the titles are *The Case of the Questionable Quadruplet, The Case of the Surly Surrogate, The Case of the Desperate Doctor* and *The Case of the Long-Lost Lover.*

You can sign up for her free newsletter and learn more about her books at her website, Jacquelinediamond.net.

If you enjoyed this novel and are willing to post a short review at your favorite online book sites, it would be much appreciated. Thank you!

www.ingramcontent.com/pod-product-compliance
Lightning Source LLC
LaVergne TN
LVHW091134080826
845145LV00008B/2155

* 9 7 8 1 9 3 6 5 0 5 7 8 4 *